The Golden Chestnut

Anna Sellberg

The Golden Chestnut

Copyright: ©Anna Sellberg 2006
Original title: Guldfuxen
Cover and inside illustrations: © 2008 Jennifer Bell
Cover layout: Stabenfeldt A/S

Typeset by Roberta L. Melzl
Editor: Bobbie Chase
Printed in Germany, 2008

ISBN: 1-933343-71-0

Stabenfeldt, Inc.
457 North Main Street
Danbury, CT 06811
www.pony.us

Chapter 1

Lori looked in the mirror and frowned. Her face was swollen from crying and her eyes were all red. Her blonde hair was lank and her bangs had turned into a mess of tangles. She shook her head and shuddered when her hands, full of cold water, reached her face.

She sighed deeply and almost started sobbing again. It was all so terrible! How could she live without Dopey? Little brown Dopey with his fuzzy ears and that glint in his eye – the most charming face in the world. He was a stubborn Gotland pony, and Lori's favorite horse at the riding school ever since she started riding three years ago. At the time she had been ten, and Dopey had been her horse for her very first lesson.

Since then, she'd been taking care of and riding him. She had been very lucky – when the first keeper got tired of Dopey and Lori had been riding for six months, she had had the chance to take care of him almost full time. For her first competition she had ridden Dopey.

Lori blew her nose and sourly looked in the mirror again. She was still all swollen from crying, and since she knew that not even more cold water would make it better, she left the bathroom and went back to her own room.

The first thing she saw was the big photo of Dopey, framed and hanging above the bed, and all at once she was crying again.

Why did it have to be Dopey? True, he was old, but he should have been allowed to live for a while longer. Lori remembered how she had been allowed to rent Dopey during the summer, and all their expeditions in the woods around her parents' summerhouse.

In spite of his twenty years, Dopey had been frisky as a young horse, and it wasn't until August, when he'd started limping a little on one hind leg, that Lori realized he was getting old.

Leonard Swanson, who owned the riding school with his wife Marianne, had come to take a look at Dopey's limping gait. He just shook his head and called a veterinarian, who came and examined Dopey. The vet had given the final verdict on Dopey's leg.

That day, Dopey had stood so obediently in the sun and allowed the vet to examine him. Lori had to swallow hard when she remembered. He had been nuzzling her hand for candy, and after Leonard and the vet had talked for a while, Leonard told Lori that there was only one solution.

Of course, Lori had pleaded and appealed, but Leonard just shook his head and opened his hands in a helpless gesture.

"His limp will only get worse and Dopey will suffer more and more. And you don't want your friend to end up like that, do you, Lori?"

Lori had desperately fought back tears. She understood. Dopey wouldn't have to suffer because of her…

"He's had a fine summer here," the vet said kindly.

Lori could only nod. With tears in her eyes, she led Dopey to the enclosed field where he'd been all summer, and then she ran sobbing down to her favorite place by the little brook that went through the field.

She'd stayed there until she was sure that both Leonard and the vet had left. She suspected that they would talk to her parents about which day Dopey would leave, but she hadn't wanted to know, not yet.

And now the day had come. Lori's family had moved home from their summer place yesterday, and today Leonard would come for Dopey.

Lori thought about yesterday. She'd stood for a long time crying with her arms around Dopey's neck, given him a lot of candy and brushed and groomed him as if he were about to enter a competition.

When it was time to leave and her mom and dad came to the field to get her, she refused to go along. Then she realized that fighting was no use. Dopey was in pain, and he would probably be even more worried with her standing there and crying.

With a big lump in her throat she hugged him one last time and then ran to the waiting car. She hadn't been able to resist turning around.

Dopey had been standing by the gate, looking after her with a big tuft of grass in his mouth. His eyes were as shiny as a young horse's when he tossed his head and trotted a few paces. Then he lowered his head and started grazing, knowing nothing about tomorrow and what would happen then.

Lori stretched out on the bed. Outside the window, the August sun was warm and the sky was clear and cloudless. She sighed deeply and turned to the wall. It was so unfair! Why Dopey? Why not some other suffering and neglected horse that nobody cared about anyway?

She heard the key in the door and then the sound of her mother coming into the hall. Lori inhaled deeply and closed her eyes. It would be nice to sleep a little. A few minutes later she was slumbering.

During dinner that night Lori was silent. She didn't eat, but just pecked at her food.

Lori's parents looked at each other. Lori seemed to be taking this Dopey business pretty well, they thought.

Lori's two-year old sister Paulina was smearing mashed potatoes all over her plate. Then she poured on lots of catsup and put her four meatballs in a nice ring in the middle.

"Can't I have a horse of my own?" Lori asked quietly, putting her fork down on the plate.

"Please, Lori, we've talked about this before. You know we don't have money for that right now."

Her mom smiled at Lori and touched her cheek.

"But it doesn't have to be that expensive," Lori protested. "We can have it at some farmer's where the stable rent is cheap, and it's all right if it's a pretty small horse, 'cause I'm only five foot three and I can still ride a pony for a long time."

Dad stroked his thin hair and sighed. He felt a little uneasy, and when he looked at his wife he sensed that she felt the same.

Lori looked at them and then down at her plate again. She swallowed and swallowed. She didn't want to cry again!

"Can't you wait for a little while?" Dad said and took a deep drink of his milk.

"But…"

Lori swallowed again.

"Yes?" her mom said and smiled encouragingly.

"If we want a stall at the riding school, there are some

free ones now," Lori said and looked up. "And it's cheaper to buy horses in the fall. It wouldn't have to cost much at all."

"I'm sorry, honey. I understand how hard it is for you to lose Dopey, but you must understand that we just can't afford it. The rent for this apartment will go up again, and everything else is getting more expensive too. Maybe if I get that part-time job at the bank that I applied for…"

Lori's mom took a deep breath and hoped silently that Lori would understand. The family had no money to spare. Right now, their budget wouldn't even manage a cheap horse and cheap stabling.

Lori nodded and looked down again. She understood that nagging was useless. Dad's police salary, even though he was a detective, was just about enough to cover their expenses; she'd heard that frequently lately.

"Maybe if I get that job," Mom repeated, trying to sound as hopeful as possible.

"New job, Mommy!" Paulina said, thrashing her spoon in her plate and making the mashed potatoes fly.

"Sure, new job," Lori's dad said morosely and wiped mashed potato from his tie.

"Paulina, why must you always make a mess?" Mom said, sounding both irritated and on the verge of laughter.

"Make a mess!" Paulina said and knocked her glass over. A river of white milk ran over the checkered tablecloth.

"Darned kid! Why can't you be good?" Lori exploded at her little sister before she quickly rose and went to her room.

"I can too be good," she heard Paulina's voice from the kitchen.

After Paulina and Lori had gone to bed that night, Lori's parents sat in the kitchen talking. No matter how they turned and stretched their family budget, it was quite impossible to raise two hundred or two hundred and fifty dollars a month for a horse.

Both Arnold and Rita sighed when they looked at the paper filled with numbers that was lying on the table. They had budgeted every item to be bought for many years to come, they didn't use the car more than they had to, and their summer place was cheap to rent and they used it a lot.

"No," Arnold said at last. He sighed and laid his pen down. "There won't be any horse for Lori right now, however much she wants one."

Rita nodded and looked at the paper. She felt so sorry for Lori.

"Maybe if I get that job," she said softly. "Let's hope for the best."

Chapter 2

School started on the third Thursday in August and Lori
felt relieved to have something to do again. During the
three days she'd been home, she'd just been thinking and
thinking about Dopey, but now, finally, she had something
new to worry about. She started the seventh grade, in a new
school with new teachers and lots of other things she'd
never experienced.

She didn't have her own desk any more, or her own
classroom. Instead she got a locker on the first floor of the
school, where she could keep all her books and clothes.

The classes were all in different rooms, and during the
first few days she spent most of her free time trying to find
the room for her next class.

Lori felt lonely in the big school. Her best friend from

grade school, Sofia, had moved during the summer and now lived in another town, several miles away. The other kids in her class were nice, but Lori missed Sofia more now than she had during the summer.

On the third day of school, right before geography class, one of her classmates who rode at her riding school came and sat with her.

"How are you?" she asked Lori, who looked up from her book.

"Oh, fine. And you?"

"You'll never guess!" Kate answered, putting her long red hair back with two barrettes.

"No, what?"

"Leonard is letting me buy Kariba!"

Kate's light blue eyes were shining with joy when she smiled at Lori.

"Oh. That's great!"

Lori smiled back. At that moment, she saw the geography teacher Mr. Hanson come strutting through the classroom door with a set of red atlases under his arm.

"Okay folks, let's start class!"

Mr. Hanson's thin voice interrupted all discussions, and Lori didn't learn all the details until lunchtime.

"Well, you see," Kate said between mouthfuls of pudding, "Mom and Dad have been promising me a horse of my own for a long time. And just recently a distant relative of Dad's up and died, and although he never met Dad we're inheriting his estate. You see, Dad was his only living relative."

Lori nodded and took another little spoonful of pudding. It was definitely not one of her favorite foods, and she almost had to force herself to swallow, although she was hungry.

"So of course I immediately phoned Leonard, and he said that if I couldn't think about any other horse than Kariba, I could buy her. She's not a very good lesson horse since she's so hot-tempered and hard for beginners to ride."

"When did you buy her?"

"Last week," Kate said, "and now I have an important question. Do you have any lease horse now, after Dopey?"

"No." Lori shook her head. "I don't. Why? You're not going to ask me to help out with Kariba, are you?"

Kate smiled and shook her head, her red hair flying.

"Oh no, I want to care for Kariba myself. But I'm going to move her to a little private stable, and there's a crossbreed there that the farmer owns. It's very nice and sweet-tempered. Yesterday, when I was there to discuss rent and so on, George Gallagher asked me if I knew anyone who would like to help him with his horse."

"George Gallagher, is that the farmer?"

"Right. A wonderful little old man, with gray hair and a moustache. He looks just like a real granddad! And he has a sweet wife who's decided to fatten me up. Every time I'm there she makes both Mom and me eat lots of cookies."

"Wow," Lori said. "But what about the horse? What breed is it?"

"You'll see," Kate said mysteriously. "Would you like to go and have a look?"

"Well…" Lori dragged the words a little. "Any chance it's a cross between an Ardennes draft horse and a Shetland pony?"

"Stop! You'll see. If you're interested, we can go there this afternoon. I'll take bus 84 from the station at quarter to four. You want to come?"

"Well, why not?" Lori said joyfully. "I'll come. But why did you ask me? Aren't you more friendly with Annie and Lisa than with me?"

"Humph," Kate snorted, standing up and taking her tray. "Annie got really weird this summer. She's going to stop riding, and it seems like she's trying hard to seem cool, so she can hang out with boys."

Lori stood up and followed Kate to the tray stand at the other end of the dining room. On her way there she saw Annie sitting with Steve and Vince, two guys in the ninth grade who were known for causing trouble. Annie was heavily made up and her dark hair was permed, standing up in all directions. She was very different from the Annie that Lori had said "have a nice summer" to a couple of months earlier.

"She's changed, hasn't she?" Kate said when she and Lori had left the dining room and were walking together toward the lockers.

"You could say that," Lori giggled.

"And Lisa," Kate said, picking up where she'd left off, "there's no use asking her. I think she's getting tired of horses and riding too. By the way, right now she's dating Pat Garrahy in 8C, and I'm not sure she'll even go on as Amigo's second keeper."

Lori nodded.

"Love, love! Sure, I'll be on bus 84 at quarter to four. Come on, we have to hurry or we'll be late for history class."

Kate was already sitting on the bus when Lori arrived, running and out of breath. Lori's bus had been late, and she thought she'd missed the 84.

The bus started moving and they were on their way. In spite of Lori's ceaseless nagging, Kate refused to say anything more about the horse.

"You'll see," was all she said, and Lori was more and more curious.

The road out to Lind Farm was winding and snaking and when they finally got off the bus Lori felt a little sick.

"It's a wonder they have buses out here at all," she said. Kate nodded.

"Yeah, but there aren't many. One in the morning and two in the afternoon, and one home at six thirty at night."

16

The girls turned onto a little gravel road, and after a while they came to Lind Farm. It was a beautiful little farm on the slope of the valley. The girls could make out the lake and the town far below, and on the other side the ground rose toward the ridge.

"You see the riding school?" Kate said, pointing.

"Is it the white house down there?" Lori said with surprise. "I didn't know it was this close."

The girls continued over to a tidy stable yard and into a small but very well kept stable. It was clean and well lit, and Lori thought she'd never seen a nicer stable. The dark brown color was rich looking and the white really white. Two of the stalls held thick layers of sun-yellow straw.

"This is great!" Lori breathed.

"Hi!" a voice behind them said.

The girls turned. In the doorway stood a little old gray-haired man with a checkered cap on his head and a happy smile on his wrinkled face.

"George Gallagher," he said, giving Lori his hand.

"Lori Berg," she said, feeling a little embarrassed.

"So you're Lori," George said. "Kate has told me about you. I hear you want a new horse to care for."

"Yes, well…"

Lori didn't really know what to say, but she and Kate followed George around the stable to a beautiful rolling field where some young horses were grazing.

"Tony! Hey, TONY!"

George's voice was loud and clear, and Lori saw something move in the shrubbery a few yards away. In a flash, a horse left the green bushes and came galloping toward Lori, George and Kate.

The gelding was maybe 61 inches high and piebald in dark brown and white. The hair in his mane and tail was black, and the fetlocks on all four legs were quite heavy. He held his noble head high, and his nostrils were wide open when he stopped in front of George, who immediately took a carrot from his pocket and gave it to him.

"Well, what do you think?" Kate looked demandingly at Lori.

"What a lovely horse! But what breed is he?"

Lori stroked Tony's neck, which was muddy and dusty with sand.

"His mom was a big New Forest pony that my daughter owned before she left home. His dad is a cross between Northern Swedish and Thoroughbred and was at the next farm for a while, but they got tired of chasing him when he would jump out of his pen and run away, so they sold him," George said, stroking the gelding's head. "There wasn't supposed to be any foal at all, but one summer day we found the stallion in Bozita's pen, and one year later this fellow arrived."

"So what happened to Bozita?" Kate asked.

"We sold her to some friends in Trenton a few years ago. Our daughter was never home to care for her, and I didn't have the time. But Tony stayed, we couldn't really sell him."

"How old is he?" Lori asked, hopelessly trying to defend herself against Tony's begging.

"He was seven this summer," George said, "so he's in his prime."

"He's lovely," Lori said. "Is he broken in?"

"Yes, but no one rides him much nowadays. It was Janet who broke him in before she went off to college."

George really sounded proud of his fine horse, and Lori understood why. Tony was a real beauty, and although she missed Dopey she felt that it would be great to take care of Tony, supposing that she'd be allowed to do it.

They walked over to the house together, where George and his wife Sarah had snacks for them. Lori instinctively felt that she'd like it here at Lind Farm.

The kitchen was clean and tidy, and there was a nice smell of freshly baked bread. The copper pans on the walls were shining, and the blonde, sturdy pine table was made for four, with lots of buns and cookies on a big plate.

"Sarah makes these wonderful buns," Kate said happily and took a cinnamon bun.

Lori still felt a little shy, but she soon took a bun too.

Mostly, she sat quietly and listened to the other three. Now and then Sarah made her take a cookie, and Lori couldn't do anything but say "Yes, please," and accept.

When Kate and Lori were picked up by Kate's father an hour later, Lori merrily announced that she'd never had better cookies in her life.

Sarah was happy and said that she'd make sure to fatten the girls up, because they were both too thin. And she invited her to come on Saturday, as they were planning a little welcome party for Kate and Kariba.

During the car ride home the girls almost talked Kate's dad's ears off, and he finally had to ask them to speak one at a time when they started to tell him what George had said about the stable and about Tony.

"You want to take care of Tony, don't you?" Kate asked Lori when her dad turned into the street with the yellow apartment buildings where Lori lived.

"Yes, absolutely! He seems like a sweetheart, and I don't think he could find a better owner."

"No, hardly!" Kate laughed. "So I'll see you in school tomorrow!"

"Right," Lori answered and jumped out of the car. "Bye!"

"Bye!"

The apartment smelled of food, and when Lori came into the kitchen after taking a shower and changing her clothes, dinner was already on the table.

"Well?" her mom said, tying a bib on Paulina, who angrily tried to get away by snaking back and forth in her chair.

"It seems great," Lori said and sat down.

"How was the horse?" her dad asked, putting a pan with grilled chicken on the table.

"He's called Tony, and he's brown and black. A gelding. The owners are named Gallagher and are very sweet. It'll be fun."

"I want to ride too!" Paulina whined, hitting her glass with her fork.

"You'll ride when you get bigger," Rita said, giving her some chunks of chicken. "You want a drumstick, Lori?"

"No thanks, actually I'm full. They treated us to snacks. Sarah bakes these wonderful buns and cookies. We ate lots."

"Oh, so that's better than real food," Arnold grumbled, frowning at Lori.

"Easy now," Rita said. "Of course Lori couldn't say no when they were treating. Here, Lori, take some chicken anyway. By the way, I'm going to the bank for an interview on Tuesday," she said, serving herself.

"That's exciting," Lori said. "Hope you get the job."

"Yes, I hope so too. I'm tired of taking care of you three. From now on, I'd like some help from you. For example, you can do the dishes tonight, Lori."

Lori sighed deeply. Do the dishes. How boring!

Chapter 3

On Saturday, Kariba moved to Lind Farm, and the horses seemed to get along fine immediately. Tony was so in love with the beautiful chestnut mare that he hardly ate all day. He just ran around Kariba with his tail in the air and his head up. The cows and calves in the field looked at the usually calm and quiet Tony with surprise. They must have wondered what was going on.

The girls were busy getting all their stuff in order in the little tack room in the stable. George had helped them find an old sofa, a little table and a braided rug, and, the girls decorated the newly painted room nicely.

Kate had brought a big poster with galloping horses from her house, and Lori had a few postcards and a poster with "The Horse's Prayer" that they put up with tacks.

On one side of the room, there were four saddle racks and some hooks for bridles and halters. The girls put their own stable boxes by that wall. While they chatted they tidied their boxes and shined up saddles and bridles.

George had come into the stable with an old worn saddle and a bridle for Tony, and the girls had to work for quite a while to clean the grime and dust from them. There were neither girth nor pad for the saddle, but Kate said that Lori could borrow the pad and girth she had brought from the riding school. She had bought some new stuff for her horse and didn't need them anymore.

Lori was thankful for this. Kate suggested that Lori try riding Tony on Sunday, and Lori felt a little nervous just thinking about it. It had been a long time since somebody had ridden Tony, and she was a little out of shape herself.

"Can you imagine, it's just a week since Dopey died," Lori said when they were done in the tack room. They were tired but happy and sat on a bench outside the stable.

"Yes, time really has rushed by. It was a good thing that I found this stable, and that there was a horse here for you to take care of."

Kate stretched and gazed at the setting sun. The air was warm, and it felt more like June than August.

"Hi, so you're ready now!" said George as he walked up to them and stopped by the bench.

"Aren't you going to see what we've done?" Kate asked and stood up.

George was very impressed with the cleaning the girls had done, and he thought it was a great idea to put the old table and sofa in the room.

"I really came to talk about something else," he said when they were back on the bench.

"And," Kate said, sounding curious. "What might that be?"

"Swanson called from the riding school. It seems he's bought a couple of horses, and at the moment he has no room for one of them. It's going to come here for a couple of weeks, maybe a month, until he's ready with the stalls in the new part of his stable."

"Great!" Kate and Lori said in unison.

"What kind of horse is it?"

Lori looked at George, who shook his gray-haired head.

"I don't know anything yet. Swanson is bringing the horse over tomorrow morning, he said. He says it's a nice horse. Some cross-breed, and the name sounded foreign."

George rose and said, "Well, I have to go to the barn. Have fun, girls!"

He raised his hand to wave and then took off.

"I wonder which horse it is?" Lori said thoughtfully.

"No idea," Kate said. "We'll see. You think Tony is bigger than Kariba? I don't. Look at them now, standing together. He must be almost 63 inches at least!"

The girls stood up and went to the pen to take a look while the sun was setting.

By ten o'clock the next morning the girls were waiting for Leonard to come with the new horse, but it was a quarter past twelve when he finally arrived with a green and white horse trailer connected to his Volvo.

"Oh, hi there!" he said when he jumped out of the car and saw the girls. "How's everything? Are you getting along with Kariba, Kate?"

"Yes, we're doing great."

Kate smiled at Leonard.

"So where's George? Oh, there you are. Hello, you old rascal!"

Leonard and George slapped each other on the back and talked for a few minutes. They had known each other for a long time, and when they were young they had gone into military service together, both in the cavalry of course. Leonard was George's opposite – tall and heavy.

"So where's this donkey you're bringing me?" George teased, turning to the trailer, which was bouncing from the movements and kicks of the impatient horse within.

"Well, heaven knows what junk I've bought," Leonard said morosely, stroking his chin.

"Oh, yeah?"

George raised his eyebrows, and Lori and Kate stared curiously at Leonard.

"Well, you can judge for yourselves. We'd better get him out quickly, before he kicks my trailer to pieces. You should have been there this morning when we got him in," Leonard went on. "We started at seven, and by half past eight we hadn't even gotten the hack up on the ramp. When we finally had him inside, the wretch rose and walked over the bar in the front of the trailer. Luckily, we have a loose bar and only have to take out a pin to take it down."

Leonard sighed and then started instructing the others on what to do. Kate and Lori had to simply keep out of the way. George had to lower the ramp, and Leonard himself had to take the lead rein and try to hold on.

"Is the safety chain on?" George asked.

"Yes, but be ready for the wretch to throw himself backwards anyway. Kate, would you get a broom? George could slap him with that and then maybe he won't throw himself out."

"That's cruel," Lori muttered while she and Kate ran into the stable to get a broom.

"Not at all," Kate protested eagerly. "It's much worse if the horse runs straight out as soon as the bar is lowered. Then accidents can really happen. George has to have a chance to release the safety chain first.

The girls gave George the broom and then stood by the

stable wall. They saw him lower the ramp, and with their hearts in their throats they could just make out a horse that was truly raging mad, throwing himself at the safety chain.

"Git!" George bellowed and slapped the horse's behind with the broom. Then he quickly opened the snap-hook that had kept the chain in place.

"Okay, HERE HE COMES!"

Leonard's voice echoed inside the trailer.

Lori and Kate watched breathlessly as a beautiful light chestnut horse threw himself out of the transport and landed sitting on the gravel. Leonard came dancing after it at full speed, and before the chestnut could do anything more, he had gotten the lead rein in a loop around its muzzle to keep the horse at bay. The excited horse didn't keep still for a second. He kept trampling around with his forelegs, neighing sharply and trying to get up.

"How about letting him loose in the pen?" George asked.

"Yes, by all means. I can't hold him for much longer."

Leonard was panting and sweating, trying to keep the horse on the ground. Over and over again, it tried to rear up and kick with its forelegs. The chestnut color shone like gold in the sun. Lori gasped for breath. She'd never before seen such a beautiful horse.

It was all Leonard could do to keep the horse under control until they were inside the gate, and as soon as he loosened the lead rein, the horse galloped wildly thru the

pen. Tony and Kariba came galloping toward the new horse and Lori heard Kate inhale sharply beside her.

"What if they fight?" she asked nervously.

"I don't think we have to worry about that," Leonard said, wiping his brow. "Geez, what an ordeal!"

"He's so beautiful," Lori said, watching the chestnut gallop through the pen.

Kariba and Tony were trying to keep up with him, and Lori was watching intently.

"What's his name?" Kate asked Leonard.

"Red Top. He's not quite a Thoroughbred, but almost. I'm going to use him as a riding school horse eventually. If that's possible," he added, shaking his head and sighing.

"How old and what breed?" George asked.

"He's five, just broken in this spring. The father is Jimmy Ripkin, a Thoroughbred racing horse. The mother originally came from England, supposedly a cross between a Thoroughbred and a Welsh Cob; a hunter in other words. I have the papers in my car."

"Where did you buy him?" Kate asked curiously.

"At Balmoral Manor. They didn't want to keep him. Their son has grown tired of horses and moved away, and their daughter doesn't dare touch the horse since she fell off him and broke her arm this summer. He's a heck of a jumper. He can fly over a yard and a half high fence like it was nothing."

"And you turned him loose in my pen!"

George almost sounded angry.

"Don't worry," Leonard laughed, "I'm sure he'll stay. If he doesn't, call me… Well, I have to get back to the riding school. Marianne's waiting. We're going down to Manchester to pick up a couple of ponies. Bye for now!"

He raised his hand in a wave, jumped into the car and drove away.

George chuckled to himself before he looked at the girls and suggested that they follow him up to the house for a snack.

The horses were calming down now, and even if Red Top still seemed nervous, he was at least grazing. But he was some distance away from Kariba, since Tony was guarding her like an angry dog guards a bone.

The girls couldn't help but admire Tony's gallantry toward Kariba. Every time Red Top came close to the mare, Tony got between them and laid his ears back. He showed in every way that he was the boss here, and that Red Top would be in trouble if he even touched Kariba.

After a long break under the garden arbor the girls thanked Sarah for everything and ran back down to the stable. It was time to try riding Tony. Lori felt butterflies in her stomach. What would happen?

"Let's just take Tony for now," Kate said. "I'll ride Kariba a little later."

"Where are we going?"

"George said that we could use the little pen behind the stable. The ground is nice and even back there, so he thought we could use it as a course. It seems his daughter used to ride there when she lived at home."

It wasn't very hard to catch Tony in the pen, but he really didn't want to follow them in. It took some time to get the thoroughly dirty horse ready, but at last Lori led a saddled Tony outside and mounted.

He was big. It was hard for Lori to get up on his back, and once there, it felt like she was sitting in the sky. Lori's heart ached when she thought about Dopey, who had been small enough for her to mount bareback just by jumping.

"Are the leathers okay?" Kate asked, trying to sound like Leonard.

"Yes, fine," Kate answered.

After tightening the girth she let Tony walk. He responded well to her aids and carefully stepped over the bars lying on the ground, and into the so-called course. Lori stroked his neck and talked to him a little, and he turned one ear back to listen to her.

"How does he feel? Is he soft?" asked Kate, climbing up on the wooden fence. She looked like a big robin in her blue riding pants and red sweater.

"Great!" Lori said happily. "Now I'm going to trot a little."

Tony seemed a little surprised at Lori's activity with her legs, and instead of trotting he just walked faster. Lori had

to slap with force and almost kick with her feet before he understood. He started trotting with rolling motions.

"Help!" Lori squealed. "I can't ride him lightly. He's taking giant leaps!"

"I'm sure you'll manage," Kate called encouragingly from the fence. "It looks good anyway."

"Thanks," Lori panted when she trotted past Kate.

After just a few circles, she slowed down to a walk again. In a while, she rode into the middle and dismounted.

"Are you quitting already?" Kate said, surprised.

"Yeah, he hasn't been walking that much lately, and I guess it's best to take it easy in the beginning. Wow, it felt weird to jump down from such a big horse."

"That's what happens when you ride ponies for too long," Kate teased.

"I think I'm going to take it easy like this for a couple of days, but next weekend let's ride out together," Lori suggested while they were leading Tony back to the pen after grooming him.

"Yes, let's. Kariba and I can ride with you during the week. I'm sure she'll need some dressage work!"

Chapter 4

The girls were in the pen all the next week and rode dressage. They helped each other, but Lori still felt hopelessly small on Tony, who at times did whatever he wanted. If he was hungry he tried to force his head down and graze on the green grass, and if he was tired of trotting he slowed to a walk and it was impossible to get him up to speed again.

"I'm going crazy," Lori moaned after riding on Friday.

"What? He's coming along nicely," Kate said with surprise. But Lori shook her head.

"He's so lazy, and nothing helps."

"You'll see, it'll get better when he gets more oats," Kate said, trying to encourage her. "We could ride out in the woods tomorrow. That'll be good for Tony."

The girls hadn't cared that much for the new horse – Red

Top – even though Lori's fingers were itching when she saw how muddy and dirty he was when he came in from the pen. George had told them to leave the gelding alone, since he wasn't quite safe.

Every night, Lori stopped for a while at Red Top's stall and talked softly to him. Sometimes he lifted his head and gave her an inscrutable look from his beautiful dark eyes, but he never came up to the door to be scratched the way Tony did.

"I can't understand why you're so fond of Red Top," Kate said when they rode the bus home on Friday night.

Lori just shrugged her shoulders. She couldn't quite explain it herself, but Red Top was one of the most beautiful horses she'd ever seen. Everything about him was so perfect: his noble head with its clear, shining white blaze that went all the way along the bridge of his nose, his long slender neck, and his dainty body. His legs were strong but slender, and Red Top always carried his long tail high like a flag when he was galloping around in the pen.

"Are we riding out tomorrow?" Lori asked when they arrived at the bus station and were walking to their different buses.

"Yeah, let's. I'll see you here at five to ten tomorrow morning!"

They parted and Lori got on her bus. Two girls from the riding school, whom she knew well from before, were already on board.

"Hi, Lori," Emma, a tall, dark-haired girl with merry brown eyes and a big smile, greeted her.

Lori went to sit in the seat in front of them. Next to Emma was a blonde girl with short hair who looked a little sullen. Her name was Marta, and she looked as if she was carrying all the troubles of the world on her shoulders.

"Hey, how are you?" Lori asked when she sat down.

"Fine," Emma said, giving Lori a searching look.

"How are things at the riding school?" Lori asked. "Are the classes starting on Monday?"

"Yes, I think so. I'm sure you've heard that there's going to be a meeting on Tuesday in the clubroom? All members are welcome."

"No, I didn't know that. What's it about?" Lori asked, looking inquiringly at her friends.

"Haven't you heard? The riding school's finances are so bad that they might have to close. Leonard might have to sell a few horses to make ends meet."

"Including Karat," Marta said angrily, making a face. "No!"

Lori looked compassionately at her. Marta had been Karat's keeper for years, ever since he came to the stable, and although the pony was almost eighteen he was still brisk and fit. If Leonard had decided to sell him, it must have more to do with his age than with his usefulness.

"That's too bad," Lori said with pity. "When will Leonard sell him?"

"As soon as possible," Marta said. "The old lady who owns Vadim is moving to a farm up north and she needs company for Vadim, so he doesn't have to be alone all the time. Leonard thinks it's best to take the chance, because other than this offer I guess nobody would want to buy Karat, except me of course."

"He'll be fine there," Lori said, trying to encourage her.

"Yes, but still. Up north, of all places!"

Marta rose to get off the bus at the next stop. Lori and Emma had a few more stops to go. They lived in the same apartment building and could go all the way home together.

"Of course we have to go to the meeting," Kate said emphatically when she and Lori met Emma, Marta, Madeline and Charlotte Ann on the bus to the riding school.

"I think all the club members are going," Madeline said, pushing her blonde bangs away from her forehead.

"I'm worried about Kola," Charlotte Ann said. "She's getting old, too. Of course, she's brisk like a young horse, but you never know."

In the avenue leading up to the riding school the girls were joined by a couple of girls on bikes and some more who were walking. The meeting room was full.

There were already lots of people in the clubroom, and Lori and Kate couldn't find a seat at any of the crowded tables. The noise level was high, but when Karl Fenton, the chairman of the riding club, came in and asked for their attention, the room became silent.

"So, this meeting is called to open," he said, banging his gavel on the table. "I'm calling upon Leonard Swanson to speak and tell us a little about what has happened during the last several weeks."

Leonard stood and cleared his throat. It felt like everybody was holding their breaths.

"As I'm sure you all know, the riding school has had financial problems for some time, and we haven't been able to solve these problems in a satisfying way," he began.

Everybody nodded.

"Karl and I," Leonard said, "have had a look at the finances. We've found that to make ends meet we have to sell a number of horses. Several of the older ones are only being used one or two hours a day, and we have to keep horses that can be used more than that."

There were whispers among the keepers, who were sitting in a group by the wall. They were worried, because the horses they were keeping might be the ones to be sold.

"Also, we have to start offering more lessons, partly by advertising in public places for people who want to start riding, partly by starting one or two more beginner's groups. We'll do that as soon as we've sold a few older horses and bought new ones. Okay, Karl, your turn."

"Right," said Karl and stood up again. "Well, we're also planning to have a *Horse Day* here at the riding school. That will give us exposure as well as money. This day will be in the middle of October, that is, in six weeks. We want to start a committee consisting both of senior and junior riders to take care of the planning. Can I have suggestions for committee members?"

Names crossed each other in the air. Lori was surprised to hear her own name, and even more surprised when she was elected.

She was close to saying no, but Kate grabbed her arm, smiled and whispered.

"It's great that you're on the committee. Now make it a fun day!"

Lori stayed seated. She was elected on the committee for the Horse Day! The meeting went on for almost another hour, and the discussion about which horses were to be sold took most of the time.

Leonard and Karl Fenton had decided that Kola, Karat and the Gotland pony Pontus would have to leave the school. Pontus wasn't well, and the other horses weren't up to being ridden more than one or two hours a day.

Instead, Leonard had been to Manchester to buy two ponies that could be ridden full-time. They were two strong

D-ponies, and they would be used for both pony lessons and riding horse lessons. The Gotland pony Pontus would probably be put down, since he had ringworm on both his hind legs. Kola and Karat were to be sold. There was already a buyer for Karat, but Kola was still for sale.

The half-breed gelding Badger was already scheduled to be put down. He had been limping for three weeks now, and wasn't getting any better. The vet had already been called.

Lori looked around. Badger's and Pontus's keepers, Charlotte Ann and Amy, looked as if they were close to tears. Lori understood how they felt. She suddenly missed Dopey, and she swallowed over and over again to keep from crying.

After the meeting, Lori and Kate went over to Leonard, who was talking to Marianne and Karl Fenton. They intended to ask about lesson times and such things, and Lori also wanted to ask Leonard what she should do about Tony.

When they came up to the group, Leonard seemed so depressed and sad that they decided to wait and call him the next day instead.

The clubroom gradually emptied, and most of the girls who were keepers went out to the stable. Lori and Kate bought a couple of candies in the snack shop and then silently sat down to eat.

Emma came to sit with them. She didn't look very happy.

41

"Poor Marta," she sighed and looked at Lori and Kate. "What would you do if you were her? She has no chance in the world of keeping Karat."

Lori shook her head.

"At least he isn't going to be put down," Kate said.

Emma nodded and rose. She was going out to watch the lesson that started at seven.

Lori and Kate looked at their watches and then slowly started walking to the bus stop. It was time to go home and do their homework.

Chapter 5

A couple of days after the big stable meeting, Lori sat on the fence of the pen and watched the grazing horses. It was Saturday, and Kate had gone away for the day, which meant that Lori, for once, was alone in the stable. At first it felt a little strange, but she quickly got used to it.

In the morning, she'd taken Tony for a long ride in the woods. Tony had been a little friskier than usual. Afterwards, she'd groomed him and brushed him until his white areas were shining. Of course, as soon as he came out of the stable he'd rolled on the ground, and now she sadly saw that he was just as dirty as before.

At that moment, Leonard's big blue Volvo drove into the yard. Lori looked at it in surprise. What could Leonard want here?

"Hi, Lori! Well, it's finally time for that rascal in the pen to pay for all the food George has given him."

Leonard smiled and handed a lead rein to Lori.

"Would you please get Red Top for me? I thought that I'd try to ride him a little today, carefully, of course."

Lori strode determinedly into the pen and managed to snap the lead rein in place below the chin of the grazing chestnut without difficulty. He seemed a little surprised, but followed Lori into the stable without protesting.

Once inside, he got a little worried and walked around his stall, neighing with his head up and his nostrils flaring.

Leonard came in with a saddle and bridle. He also carried a couple of brushes.

"Is Red Top really going to be a lesson horse?" Lori asked while Leonard brushed mud and dust from the horse.

"No, probably not. I've had a great offer from James Gruenwald. His daughter needs a new competition horse since her pony is now too small."

"Oh," Lori said, a little sadly.

She knew Isabelle Gruenwald all to well. Isabelle was the most boastful and snobbish student in the entire riding school. Isabelle found faults everywhere and taunted everybody about their riding. She always wore expensive designer clothes, even in the stable, but of course she never did any stable work herself.

Lori had heard that at home, in Isabelle's dad's own

stable, she had three or four younger girls who had to do all the work: mucking out, saddling and bridling. Isabelle herself just mounted and rode.

"When does she want him?" Lori asked slowly. She watched Leonard saddle and bridle the chestnut gelding, which wasn't still for a moment.

"She'll come to get him in about two weeks. Until then, he'll stay here, and I'll come here to ride him every day. Actually, he's a nice little horse. I've been riding him almost every morning all this week. And he learns quickly and is very eager."

"How much are they paying you for him?" Lori looked inquiringly at Leonard.

"Almost eight thousand dollars," he said and led the saddled horse out in the passageway.

Lori watched silently while Leonard mounted Red Top and rode toward the woods. Eight thousand dollars! What an enormous amount of money. Lori sighed deeply. She knew that she'd never get a horse like Red Top, never in a million years.

"Think about that, Tony," she said, stroking the gelding's head when he came up to the fence to beg for candy and a scratch. "To have a horse like that, a noble horse that does what one asks of him … the best would be a Thoroughbred, no, the best would be Red Top. You're okay too, Tony, but I wish I had some money."

"Eight thousand dollars!" Kate squealed on the phone that evening. "No wonder Leonard is selling him."

"True, but I'm not too happy that it's Isabelle Gruenwald who's buying him. There are so many *good* riders around here."

"Yes, that's true. The question is if Isabelle can manage a horse that difficult. She couldn't manage that spirited competition pony they bought for her."

"Red Top isn't difficult," Lori defended her favorite horse, "he learns quickly and he's eager, or so Leonard told me."

"Well, we'll see. I have to get back to geography. You started yet?"

Lori said no, and after chatting about school for a while the two girls hung up. Lori rose and went into the living room, where Mom was sitting sewing a playsuit for Paulina.

"My, you look sad, Lori. What's up?"

"You know that beautiful chestnut, Red Top? He's been sold to a girl named Isabelle Gruenwald. She's terribly stuck up, and I feel so sorry for him."

Lori sighed and sat down in a chair. Her mom stopped sewing and looked up.

"But you have Tony to take care of, so you don't have to worry about that. I'm sure it'll be okay."

"I don't know. Red Top is so beautiful," Lori said dreamily. "Just the kind of horse I'd want, noble and beautiful and a little more eager than Tony. Tony's so lazy when you ride him!"

"Okay," Rita said and went on sewing, "but you know it's impossible."

"I know," Lori muttered. "Do you know how much Leonard got for Red Top?"

"No. I actually have no idea, I know nothing about what horses are worth."

"Almost eight thousand dollars."

Lori's mom was surprised.

"That much for a horse? Is that so?"

"Yes," Lori said. "I'm afraid it is so. I guess Leonard just had to sell Red Top. The riding school has a lot of debts that have to be paid and Isabelle's dad is paying for a part of the new riding school building. If Isabelle isn't allowed to buy Red Top, he might change his mind, and then the riding school will go bankrupt. What's the time, by the way? There's a horse show on TV at seven."

"It's five to seven, so you'd better turn it on now."

The following Tuesday, Isabelle Gruenwald and her dad came up to Lind Farm with Leonard. It was time for Isabelle to try riding Red Top. Lori and Kate gave each other a look. To celebrate the day, Isabelle was dressed in white riding pants and a lamb's wool sweater from the most expensive shop, and her long, blonde hair was in two braids.

Isabelle didn't even look at Lori and Kate, although they'd known each other for years. Isabelle was one year older than Lori and Kate, and they'd been in the same group a couple of times when they rode ponies.

Lori almost gritted her teeth when she saw how Lori fawned on Leonard, who didn't seem to notice. He smiled and talked to James Gruenwald, who was panting in the September sun. Mr. Gruenwald was a fat man with thin hair and a suit that was as well-tailored as his black shoes were shiny.

Leonard asked Lori to get Red Top, and she did. The horse wasn't difficult to catch, but he didn't really want to come inside the stable. Leonard saddled and bridled him in the blink of an eye and then led Red Top out to Isabelle, who was outside the stable, chatting to her dad.

"But what about my helmet? Can you get it from the car, Dad?"

Isabelle got her father going, and while he was getting the helmet she adjusted the leathers and mounted. Her father came panting with the helmet and a long crop, and Isabelle got Red Top to walk and followed Leonard, who was heading toward the riding course.

Lori and Kate padded after them. Lori felt cold in her stomach.

During the first circles Red Top walked without any problem, but when Isabelle drove him to a trot, they didn't look perfect anymore. Isabelle wasn't really a good rider, and when she rode lightly she thudded down in the saddle, pulling on Red Top's mouth. The gelding walked with his head high, taking short, tripping steps. He wasn't comfortable at all, Lori saw at once.

Isabelle sat down in a short trot, and now her hands were going back and forth and up and down even more. She kept pulling at Red Top's mouth the whole time. Lori saw Leonard open his mouth to tell Isabelle to keep her hands still, but at that moment James Gruenwald smiled contentedly and said, "There, no problems at all! Well, I suppose the girls have to have real riding horses when they get older. A pony won't do for long."

Leonard seemed to swallow what he had to say and just nodded.

Lori and Kate looked at each other. Red Top really didn't walk well for Isabelle. It was strange that James Gruenwald knew too little about horses to even notice.

"Oh, what a lovely horse!" Isabelle said, pulling Red Top up right in front of her dad and Leonard.

"Does he feel all right, little Isabelle?" Gruenwald asked.

"Does he! He's just the kind of hot and fiery horse that I've always wanted! We *are* buying him, aren't we, Dad?"

"Sure, if you want him."

"When do you want to take him home?"

Leonard looked inquiringly at Gruenwald.

"As soon as possible," he said, rubbing his fat hands together and smiling. "Of course, I'll pay cash when we come for him. Jump down now, Isabelle, I think Mom has dinner ready at home."

Isabelle dismounted and threw the reins to Lori, who was closest. Leonard looked at Lori and smiled.

"Will you please take him in and care for him?" he asked Lori. "That's very kind of you."

"Of course the girl will take care of the horse," James Gruenwald interrupted loftily and threw Lori a glance. "Well, go on! It's not good for the horse to stand still when he's warm."

Lori led Red Top back to the stable, and behind her she heard Leonard and Mr. Gruenwald close the deal. A vet would examine Red Top as soon as possible. Leonard would try to get the vet to come the next day.

Lori suffered when she heard Isabelle talking about Red Top as if he was already her horse. She sighed and led Red Top into his stall. A few minutes later, she heard Leonard's car start as he left for the riding school.

"Not that I want to be picky," Lori said to Kate who had come in and was sitting on the big oats box, "but he really walked badly, didn't he? Poor horse, that's all I've got to say!"

Kate nodded. She agreed with Lori. Red Top really was too fine a horse for Isabelle Gruenwald.

"Poor Red," Lori said, affectionately stroking the gelding's neck since she had unsaddled him. "You would have been better off at Leonard's school than with that ape."

"Bad luck," Kate said, shrugging her slender shoulders.

"This horse really has bad luck. Lori, are you going to the riding school tomorrow to practice with the quadrille riders?"

"Right, tomorrow's Wednesday. Yes, I'm going. If you like, maybe you could ride Tony a little tomorrow. Wouldn't that be fun, as a change from your usual madcap rides?"

"If I have the time," Kate laughed as she rose, "but thanks for the offer. Look, I think Dad's actually coming to get us. Hurry up with Red Top, if you can."

Lori brushed quicker and then let Red Top out into the pen. He immediately rolled lustily, and she couldn't help smiling to herself. He looked so funny, lying on his back with all four legs in the air, the dry dust in the horses' favorite hollow flying around him. It wasn't until Kate called for her from the car that she hurried away to go home.

Chapter 6

"I think we'll have Amor and Julie as the first couple, and Tin-Tin and Ruffen as the second."

Lori looked around the indoor ring where the pony riders who'd been selected for the quadrille walked around in the square.

Madeline on Julie rode up to Anya and Amor. The two dark brown mares looked good together. Behind them, Caroline and Emma followed suit on Ruffen and the gray Tin-Tin. Although Ruffen was a light cream color, the two went well together.

Lori thought for a while and then chose Marta and Lisa on the two Welsh Cobs, Tanja and Pluto as couple number three, and for the fourth couple Linda and Hanna on the two Gotland ponies Klara and Linette.

Lori thought about it again, but this seemed to be the most elegant way to place the very different ponies together.

Leonard, who was testing the speaker system, called down to Lori from his booth and asked if she was ready. Lori hollered a "Yes" back to him.

"Do you know the program?" she asked the eight pony riders. A few of them nodded while the others shook their heads.

"I don't know it," Hanna squealed from Linette's back.

"We know it pretty well," Madeline said, gesturing toward Anya and Amor. "If we ride first, I'm sure it'll work out."

"I'm starting the music!"

Leonard's music interrupted all further discussion when the strands of a well-known military march boomed from the speakers.

The horses pricked their ears, and Julie and Amor, the two ponies from Manchester, shied back a little. They soon got used to it, and when Lori commanded a short trot, everybody got moving.

Lori started with an ordinary lesson. The riders got to practice riding in pairs, changing hands across the diagonal and changing hands through the middle of the school. It turned into a bit of a mess, and there were moments of utter chaos, but finally the girls understood what they had to do and started practicing the program in earnest.

At the very moment when all eight horses and riders

turned across to the gallery to practice the first halt, Isabelle Gruenwald and her parents entered the riding school. Lori looked at them with surprise. The stable was actually closed now, and there wasn't supposed to be any audience for the quadrille practice.

Lori tried to ignore the three people standing on the gallery and talking to Leonard. She called out for a short trot and tried to get the girls to ride the program as well as possible.

Of course there was chaos. The girls rode the wrong way and Lori sighed hopelessly. Once again, she commanded the horses and riders to ride up the middle line, turn up toward the gallery, and then start a short trot again.

This time it worked well for a while, but then Tin-Tin got scared by a stable cat that jumped from the sideboards down into the ring. Tin-Tin shied back violently and Emma had to fight to stay in the saddle. Before she knew what was happening, Tin-Tin had thrown her into the sawdust and was trotting around with his reins hanging.

"Are you hurt?" Lori called to her friend, who immediately stood up.

"Of course not," Emma exclaimed, "but I have sawdust everywhere!"

While Lori went to catch Tin-Tin, Emma brushed herself off as well as she could, and she was soon back in the saddle.

"Let's do it again," Lori ordered, and all the horses and riders organized themselves once again.

A little while later, Tin-Tin got scared and shied again. This time, Emma managed to stay in the saddle, but the horse still caused great confusion in the rows before Emma got him back in place again.

"Take it from the top!" Lori sighed wearily and looked at her group.

"Hey, Lori, can you come up here for a minute?" Leonard called.

Lori jogged up to the gallery, where Leonard and the Gruenwald family were standing. The girls and horses in the ring got to walk around with long reins and relax for a while.

"Yes, what's up?" Lori asked.

"What do you think about the quadrille practice?" Leonard asked with a smile.

"Well, considering it's the first time, not bad," Lori said and looked at him.

She smelled a rat. She suspected that Isabelle wanted to take over the quadrille practice.

"I don't think it's going that well," Mrs. Gruenwald said loftily and tightened her mink coat around her.

"Well, you can't expect that much the first time," Lori said and smiled at her.

"I really don't think it's acceptable," James Gruenwald said haughtily, "that such a young and inexperienced girl as you is responsible for a difficult matter such as this. What

58

if the quadrille is a failure? On Horse Day, the honor of this riding school will be at stake."

Lori blushed and looked sternly at Mr. Gruenwald.

"I can't really see what my age has to do with that," she growled, "and by the way, I'd better continue now, but thanks for your support."

Lori was as mad as a hornet, and she turned and stomped back down to the ring. She commanded a short trot, and then she asked the girls to make rows of two and two. She was angry enough to want to scream, and she could still hear the Gruenwalds discussing the quadrille with Leonard.

"Turn up toward the gallery and start riding the program," Lori said to the girls, who immediately obeyed.

This time the girls gave it their all, and although the group hadn't made it through the program even once before, everything went well this time. Everybody did their best, and when they rode up for the final halt Lori let out her breath. She felt weak in the knees, and noticed that she had been clenching her fists tight enough to turn her knuckles white.

"That was great," she praised the girls and proudly turned to the gallery, but neither Leonard nor the Gruenwalds were there. With the military march still booming from the speakers Lori asked the girls to take in and groom the horses. They were done. She praised them again and asked them to study the program for next time. If they did that she was sure everything would work out fine.

Lori went directly out to the bus when she was done. She didn't pass the clubroom and the office. Gruenwald's big, silvery Mercedes was still out in front of the stable, and there was a horse trailer connected to it.

Suddenly she realized that the Gruenwalds might be picking Red Top up today, if he had passed the vet's examination. Lori felt her heart jump in her chest. Maybe they had already picked him up?

She jumped up and down impatiently as she waited for the bus, and when it finally arrived the driver went so slow that she wished she could take over the driving herself.

She was lucky and made it to the police headquarters just before her father's shift ended, and with some persuasion he agreed to drive her to the stable.

Lori smiled gratefully at him and jumped into the family's little red car, which was parked in front of the police building.

It was already getting dark although it was only seven o'clock, and Lori thought about the fact that it would soon be totally dark by four in the afternoon.

Lori hurried to the paddock as soon as she got out of the car, but there were only two horses there: Tony and Kariba. Tony trotted up to the fence and begged for candy, and Lori stroked him a little absently. Had they already left with Red Top? Or could he be down in the shrubs, grazing by himself?

She ran down to check, but Red Top wasn't there. The cows and calves looked at her with surprise, and even Tony and Kariba kept their eyes on her.

Although Lori tried to tell herself that Red Top was in his stall inside the stable, she knew he had already left. She felt a strange regret. Red Top had never shown any appreciation when she stroked him or talked to him. She had never ridden him, and she hadn't even taken care of him during the three weeks he had been at Lind Farm.

She ran into the stable, but it was empty. Red Top's stall was cleaned and scrubbed and Lori realized that George must have taken care of it as soon as Red Top left.

She slowly walked out to the yard, where her father was talking to George.

"Well, Lori, he's gone…"

George looked at Lori and smiled sadly.

"Too bad you didn't get to say goodbye to him," Lori's dad tried to comfort her.

Lori looked up.

"Yes, it is too bad," she admitted, "but after all, Red Top is just a horse, even if he is a very beautiful horse…"

Lori went to the car, called goodbye to George, and they drove home. It was very quiet in the car and Lori sat looking out the window.

"It looks like Mom's getting that part-time job," Lori's dad said after a while.

"Oh," Lori said and nodded, "that must be fun for her."

"Then maybe we can afford a horse for you. I just spoke to George about Tony. He's a nice horse, isn't he?"

"Tony? I don't think George will sell him, and anyway I'm not sure that I want Tony."

"Why don't you want Tony? He's calm and nice, right?"

"I like Tony a lot," Lori tried to explain, "but I don't want him for my own. He isn't my dream horse."

"Sometimes I don't understand you at all," Lori's dad sighed, shaking his head. "You've been nagging us about a horse of your own for years, but when I suggest a good horse that Mom and I could possibly buy for a decent price, you don't want it!"

They fell silent again. Neither Lori nor Arnold had anything more to say. It wasn't until they were back in town that Arnold spoke.

"So what's so special about this Red Top, or whatever he's called?"

Lori sighed. She knew that she couldn't explain what was special about him. She had ridden a lot of horses, she had been Dopey's keeper and she still missed him, and right now she was taking care of a decent horse that she liked a lot.

"I don't know," Lori answered truthfully at last. "That's just the way it is."

Her father sighed again and parked the car outside their house. He couldn't understand what was wrong with Lori. She really had changed in the last few weeks.

As soon as Lori and Arnold walked through the door, Rita came up to them with an envelope in her hand. She was beaming with happiness and her cheeks were red.

"I got the job!" she said joyfully.

"Congratulations, Mom!" Lori said, and hugged her before going to her room to change clothes.

"Yes, this really is great," Arnold said, hugging his wife and kissing her cheek.

"I've bought roast beef and made potato salad for dinner," Rita said, "and I also baked a cake for dessert."

Lori heard her parents go into the kitchen, and with clean clothes over her arm she padded across the hall and into the bathroom to take a shower.

She was glad that her mother had gotten the job. She was also happy that she would get her own horse, but she didn't want Tony. She wanted Red Top, or a horse just like him.

She understood that it would be some time before the family could afford such a horse, and in that case it might be better to wait. For now, she had Tony to ride and take care of at no cost, which was great.

After dinner the family plopped down in front of the TV, and when the news ended Arnold switched off the set and turned to Lori.

"Well, have you thought about what we talked about in the car?"

"Oh," Rita said, pretending to be angry, "you've told her already?"

"You mean about buying a horse?" Lori said, smiling.

"Right," Rita said joyfully and hugged Lori's slender shoulders. "What do you say? Wouldn't that be something? We're going to have just enough money now to afford a pony or a little horse for you. I know how much you've been longing for that. Both dad and I have been wanting to buy you a horse for a long time, but we haven't been able to afford it, as you know."

"Yes, I know," Lori said and smiled again.

She didn't know what to say. Her parents were the best in the world and it was terrific that they really wanted to give her a horse. She knew that they'd still have to scrounge a little, in spite of Rita's new job and salary.

But still, she didn't want to. Somehow, she felt all wrong inside when she merrily said, "This is the best thing that's ever happened," and that she would "buy a horse magazine first thing tomorrow and start looking through the ads."

"It can't be that expensive," Arnold said when he heard Lori's plan.

"How much can we spend?" Lori asked.

"Well, no more than three thousand dollars. We have to use our savings, and they're not that big."

Lori nodded. It was as she had thought. Twenty thousand wouldn't even be enough for half of the kind of horse she wanted, but she was still overjoyed that her parents had changed their minds at last. She was really, finally, going to get her own horse!

Chapter 7

"That's great!" Kate exclaimed when Lori told her. "Congratulations!"

Lori nodded and smiled. It really was great, and now that she'd had the time to think a little about it, she felt that, after all, it wouldn't be too bad to own a horse that might not be as expensive and fine as Red Top. On the contrary, a little crossbreed without papers or pedigree might be just as nice.

"When will you start looking?" Kate said as the girls rode the bus to the stable in the afternoon.

"As soon as the next issue of that magazine with all the horse ads is out," Lori said. "It's going to be so exciting, don't you think?"

"Are you going to ask anyone who knows more than you to come along and look at the horses?" Kate asked.

"Yes, I'm going to ask Leonard and Marianne if one of them has the time to come along. I guess that's the best plan. I don't know enough to go by myself."

"Sounds smart," Kate said. "Can I come along?"

"Of course," Lori said. "C'mon."

The September wind was cold and it was drizzling, so the girls almost ran all the way to the farm. They could really feel that fall was coming now, and Lori shuddered when she thought about how it would soon be dark when they got to the stable in the afternoons. She was afraid of the dark, and she knew that Kate was, too, even if she didn't admit it.

George had already taken in both horses, and once they saw the stalls the girls knew that he'd mucked out, too.

"How great that that's done," Kate said happily. "Now we can ride right away. Hurry up, so we can get out before it's pitch dark."

"Do you have any reflectors?" Lori asked.

Kate shook her red-blond head and sighed.

"No, I don't, actually, but there are never any cars on this gravel road, are there?"

"But what if…"

Lori looked at Kate.

"Oh, you're always so silly."

"Silly? Just because I worry about Tony and me?" Lori said angrily.

The two girls stood on each side of the passageway, glaring fiercely at each other. Lori was hot with anger and she could see that Kate was mad as well.

She angrily turned on her heel and went in to brush Tony. As usual, he greeted her by butting her in the tummy, begging for candy.

Lori was done first and, with her nose in the air, she went into the tack room for Tony's gear and started tacking him. Kate was free to ride out if she liked, but Lori was going to ride dressage behind the stable.

Tony seemed quite surprised when Lori led him toward the paddock at the same time Kate sat up on Kariba and rode along the gravel road that led to the riding school. Lori was still irritated as she rode, and Tony, who could sense her anger, performed worse than ever.

Lori tried to get him to walk properly, but he just yanked his head up and refused to work. He didn't even want to do leg-yieldings, something he was usually good at.

After less than half an hour, Lori gave up. Working this way was useless, she knew. She angrily rode up to the front of the stable and dismounted.

"Darn horse, stand still!" she roared at Tony, who started walking toward the stable door before she had finished running up the stirrups.

As soon as Tony went into his stall he started to eat, and

Lori sourly smacked him on his neck. He would have to wait until she got his bridle off.

Tony didn't understand a thing. He gave Lori a surprised look from his dark eyes and for a moment Lori's conscience really bothered her. It wasn't Tony's fault that she had quarreled with Kate and was in a bad mood.

"Hey, you big ape," she softly whispered in Tony's ear.

She gave him a piece of carrot to beg forgiveness for being unkind.

"Isn't it weird?" she whispered to the horse. "Here I am, being promised a horse of my own, and I should really be terrifically happy and grateful. Instead, I fight with Kate and am mean to you. You'll see, I won't get any horse at all after…"

Lori's thoughts were interrupted when Tony quickly lifted his dark head and pricked his ears. His eyes were shining, and suddenly he neighed sharply. Lori couldn't understand what was the matter with him, but she stroked his neck and talked softly to him. She suspected that he had reacted to the wind outside, which was getting worse and worse. It actually sounded as if the first fall storm was coming.

To be really sure that nothing was wrong Lori went to the door and looked out. In the next moment, she shied back in fear. Outside the door was Kariba, with her saddle empty, reins hanging and blood on one foreleg. It was almost impossible to see in the darkness, so Lori opened the door wide and led the mare into the passageway.

Tony neighed quietly to his friend, who just pricked her ears in answer. Kariba was a mess: her reins were trampled, blood was trickling from her mouth, she was covered in mud, and she had blood on her chest and right side. Her saddle was at an angle, and the left stirrup was gone.

"But what…" Lori swallowed. "Where's Kate? What happened?"

She quickly led Kariba into her stall and ran up to the house. She hoped that somebody would be home, but the place was dark and quiet.

What can I do? Lori thought in despair. Maybe Kate is lying somewhere along the road, badly hurt. I have to ride out and try to find her! If I only knew which way she went.

Lori's heart was pounding wildly and thoughts were careening through her head while she quickly got a saddle and bridle on Tony and took him out into the passageway. She tried to stuff the bottle of iodine, some cotton and two elastic bandages into her jacket pockets and, luckily, finally managed. Her throat was dry when she led Tony out in the yard.

It was almost dark out now. The wind was strong, and the drizzle stubbornly continued. Lori folded up her rain jacket collar and struggled up onto Tony's back.

Tony shook his head in irritation. He really wanted to go back into the nice warm stable again, back to the hay and oats that he knew would soon be served. He didn't want to leave the yard at all, and when Lori signaled him, he went backwards instead of forwards.

"Forward! Just walk!" Lori roared and hit him on the neck with the end of the reins.

Very unwilling, Tony started walking down the gravel road toward the riding school. Lori wasn't sure that was where Kate had gone, but she hoped so with all her heart.

The rain came down heavier and Lori shuddered when she left the safe circle of light from the lamp above the stable door. The light didn't reach down to the road, and it was pitch black all around her. Tony walked very reluctantly, with his ears pinned angrily back. He wanted to go home.

Lori pulled her raincoat closer around her and got Tony to trot. It was very dark and the fields had been replaced by forest on both sides. There was no light anywhere. Lori was worried that a car would come. She had no reflector pads, either on the horse or on herself. She hoped that the white patches on Tony and her own white raincoat would make them at least a little visible.

All the time, she worried about Kate. What had happened? Had Kariba been scared and thrown Kate off somewhere? But in that case, why was Kariba all muddy and smeared with blood? Had she fallen?

Lori nervously clenched her jaw and stared as hard as she could to try to see anything through the falling rain. The road snaked on, and there were squelching and splashing sounds as Tony plowed through the pools of water that had already formed.

"Hey! KATE!"

Lori called as loudly as she could, but there was no indication that anybody had heard her. She called over and over again, but the only sounds reaching her ears were from Tony and her squelching raincoat. Lori slowed the horse to a walk so she could hear better.

Suddenly she saw a pair of headlights come around a bend in the road further down, and she looked ahead with fear. Right here, the road was narrow and the woods were thick on both sides. There was nowhere she could go to shelter herself and Tony from the car. What could she do?

The car came closer and closer, its headlights blinding both her and the horse.

"Down into the ditch, Tony! Hurry!"

Lori pushed Tony on and made him take a couple of steps down into the ditch and up to the edge of the woods. The ground was slippery and wet, but Tony obediently stopped. Lori held her breath as the car came closer.

The headlights dimmed and the car slowed down. Apparently, the driver had seen her. She breathed a sigh of relief. Tony didn't seem to care about the car. He stood calmly chewing on a branch that he found.

A moment later the car stopped and Kate jumped out. When the light inside the car went on Lori could see that the driver was Leonard, and the car was his big Volvo.

"Lori! What are you doing here? Where's Kariba?"

Kate was worried.

"Kariba is back home in her stall, but what about you? How are you? What happened?"

"Girls, let's try to get home as quickly as possible. Kate, get in the car. We'll drive behind Lori so she can see."

Leonard's voice made the girls jump, and they obeyed immediately. With the car behind her, Lori had no problem trotting all the way home. The headlights lit the road and Lori saw every treacherous hole. Her legs were trembling and tired from tension. It had been so ghostly, quiet and dark, with the rain just falling and falling.

Finally, she turned into the yard, and before she'd even dismounted Kate was on her way in to Kariba, with Leonard one step behind. Lori drew a deep breath and led Tony in. She was glad it was all over. She felt sick from the tension that had held her for the last half hour.

"She seems to have made it without being hurt too badly," Leonard said as he examined Kariba.

Kate washed the mare with lukewarm water and, luckily, the horse seemed to have suffered just small scratches and surface wounds.

"What happened?" Lori asked when she'd unsaddled

Tony and laid a blanket across his back, with lots of straw under him.

"I really don't know," Kate said truthfully. "We were trotting along the road from the riding school, and suddenly Kariba threw herself into the ditch and fell over. It all happened so quickly that I didn't even see what frightened her."

"Probably a deer," Leonard said thoughtfully, nodding to himself.

"I was lucky after all. I got thrown off and landed not too far from Kariba, so I didn't get hurt. But she didn't get up right away and I was really scared. And when I walked up to her to take her reins, she threw herself up and bolted off.

Lori nodded and, while pouring oats for Tony and Kariba, Kate went on with her story:

"At first I tried calling her, but I realized she wouldn't care, so I ran back to the riding school and asked Leonard for help. I was scared to death the whole time, because Kariba had no reflectors, and if she'd met a car at that speed she'd couldn't have jumped to the side and she'd have been run over."

"But why on Earth didn't you two go riding together?" Leonard grumbled.

"I didn't want to ride out because it was so dark," Lori said quietly, feeling responsible for the whole thing.

"It was all my fault," Kate said, sounding close to

tears, "I shouldn't have left on my own. And definitely not without reflectors."

"No, that was unusually stupid," Leonard said harshly.

Kate nodded and swallowed.

"But now you've learned your lesson," Leonard said in a somewhat friendlier voice.

Kate looked up.

"You can be sure I'm going to get some reflectors and a headlamp, or something like that. Or maybe just stay at home with Kariba until next spring."

"Yeah, I sure hope so." Lori shuddered. "It was terrible out there when Tony and I were looking for you."

"It was so nice of you to go looking," Kate said in a friendly voice. "I'm sorry for acting that way before."

"Well, girls, I've got to get back to the riding school and feed my horses. By the way, Lori, we're rehearsing the quadrille again tomorrow night at eight. You're coming?"

"Of course," Lori said.

"What should I do about Kariba if she's limping tomorrow?"

Kate affectionately stroked her beloved horse on the head.

"Call me and I'll come have a look," Leonard decided.

Then he said goodbye and left to go home.

He'd just disappeared when George's car turned into the yard. A moment later, both Sarah and George came into the stable.

"What was Leonard doing here?" George said in a curious tone.

"Well," both Kate and Lori said at once before falling silent again.

"The thing is…" Kate began.

In a few minutes, George had heard the whole story. He didn't look very happy, but he didn't seem as angry as Leonard.

"You'll be careful from now on, won't you?" Sarah said tensely to Lori and Kate, who nodded in unison.

Absolutely!

Chapter 8

There were private lessons at the riding school on Saturday, and both Lori and Kate were there with their horses. There were also four somewhat older riders and Isabelle Gruenwald on Red Top.

Lori's heart jumped when she saw the Gruenwald's horse trailer outside the stable. Now she'd finally get to see how Red Top was doing. She'd been thinking about him now and then during the almost three weeks since he'd left, but just as with Dopey's death, it all felt so far away.

When she saw the ragged and thin horse that had been a shining golden chestnut with proud stature and happy eyes, she almost cried. How could anybody destroy a horse that way?

Kate just shook her head when she saw Red Top, and she tried in vain to get Lori to think about something else while they were leading their horses around outside the stable, waiting for the lesson. Lori walked silently with Tony. She stared down at the ground, and over and over again she had to swallow to keep from crying. She had a big lump in her throat.

The lesson started and Lori tried to see as much as she could of how Isabelle was handling Red Top. She could see that Isabelle had problems with the chestnut, since he had a Pelham with long leg aids and also a martingale fixed to his noseband.

"To begin with, you have to get the martingale off Red Top," she heard Leonard say to Isabelle.

Isabelle protested strongly.

"I can't hold him if I do! He goes wild and just throws his head. You can't imagine how disobedient he's gotten in just a couple of weeks!"

"Take the martingale off," Leonard said curtly.

Isabelle dismounted and removed it, looking very angry.

Lori saw Kate smile maliciously, and she wanted to smile herself. That served Isabelle right!

The lesson started with a warmup, and Lori had to fight a lot with Tony, who was in his laziest mood. She had the hardest time getting him to trot, and it didn't help much when Lori used her crop now and then to push him on. To put it bluntly, Tony wasn't the right horse for this kind of activity. Lori understood that right away.

Lori was so lost in her own thoughts as she was riding that she came close to colliding with Isabelle and Red Top. It wasn't until Isabelle yelled at her to "watch out with that stupid circus horse" that Lori woke and gave Isabelle a mean look.

"No fighting!" Leonard said and kept on building obstacles.

They were asked to ride a figure eight over four hurdles. Lori felt her stomach tingle. She wasn't all that fond of jumping, even if it felt good when everything went right.

Lori remembered the first time she had jumped with Dopey and how he had stopped and thrown her off after the obstacle. She had cried and refused to get up again.

She hadn't dared trying again until Marianne promised on her honor that Dopey would never do it again. And the next time, there had been no problems.

"Okay, let's start with Evan and Mistral, please."

Lori watched admiringly as Evan rode his big competition horse Mistral around the course in a perfect figure eight, round and even. Evan and his big half-blood almost flew over each jump effortlessly. Lori sighed deeply. She'd never be able to ride that well.

After three figure eights Evan and his horse were done, and then Leonard said that it was Lori's turn. She would have preferred to jump a little later, but she had no choice.

She nervously made Tony gallop and went for the first two fences.

Full stop!

Lori crawled back into the saddle and straightened her helmet, which had gone down over her face. Behind her, she heard Isabelle giggling sharply and loudly.

"Come on now, Miss Berg," Leonard said, smiling. "That wasn't very good."

Lori smiled back and got Tony galloping again. This time, she rode a warm-up turn in slow canter before going for the fences again. She sensed that Tony was going to refuse again, but a couple of strong leg aids got him over the fence. Unfortunately, he happened to lose his rhythm and took fence number two in such a strange way that Lori lost her balance and slid off into the sawdust.

At first, she just lay still, staring at the ceiling.

This isn't happening to me, she slowly thought while standing up to remount. Leonard came walking with Tony, who happily nudged her for a piece of carrot.

The other riders looked amused and Isabelle made a sarcastic remark about people on circus horses usually not falling off.

Lori was as mad as a hornet when she mounted Tony. This time, she felt, it was a matter of jumping or dying. Isabelle wouldn't get another chance to laugh at her.

"Don't you act up now, you wretch!" she hissed at Tony and gave him active aids for all she was worth.

Tony came in quickly this time and took both obstacles

elegantly. He went high over them and his jumps were so long and smooth that Lori didn't really know how it had happened.

Her face red with exertion, Lori drove Tony toward the next pair of fences in a smooth turn, and a miracle occurred; Tony jumped beautifully this time.

Leonard called out "GREAT!" with feeling, and Lori was relieved when she slowed down and walked Tony to the track where the riders waiting to jump were hanging out.

Now it was Isabelle's turn, and Lori couldn't help hoping that she would fall off, at least once. One shouldn't really be that mean with people, but she couldn't resist hoping a little. Isabelle's comments about Lori's "circus horse" had made her angry.

Tony couldn't help that he wasn't the best riding horse in the world. He was a great pal and the best paddock horse in the world, but he would probably never achieve greatness either in jumping or dressage.

Isabelle galloped a couple of turns with Red Top. Lori couldn't understand why she had the martingale on the chestnut gelding, since he went with his head low and almost all his weight on his forelegs instead of his hind legs, where the weight should be.

Isabelle sat leaning back with her hands high to try to lift the entire front of the horse, and when she had galloped a little more than one turn, she slowed to a trot and happily called to Leonard, "You have to admit that he's working nicely now."

Lori didn't hear Leonard's answer, but she could tell by his expression that he wasn't very happy with the rider and horse in front of him. The way Red Top looked now, he was miles away from the shining, well-kept horse that Leonard had sold to Isabelle three weeks earlier.

"You can ride now," Leonard said.

Isabelle galloped Red Top and drove him toward the first fence. The horse galloped clumsily and just made it over, and Isabelle, losing her balance, pulled sharply at his mouth. Red Top threw his head up to get away from the pain, and by knocking down heavily with his forelegs, he managed the second fence without falling.

Isabelle came down on his back with a heavy thud and Red Top moaned as if the air was knocked out of him. Isabelle's jerky hand movements made him throw his head around all the way to the next two fences.

Lori could have killed Isabelle right then when she saw how she was treating Red Top, but she sat on Tony, powerless with anger, and walked him around in small circles. There was nothing she could do or say. There was nothing in the world that could save Red Top from Isabelle.

The next two fences were a little better and Leonard

commanded "slower." Red Top stumbled when he changed to trot and Isabelle pulled sharply at his mouth again.

"He's limping!" Lori called out loudly.

It was true, Red Top was walking with a limp. He was indicating clearly with his right foreleg.

"You're right," Leonard said quickly. "Dismount, Isabelle, and let me examine his leg."

"Oh, never mind that! He just does that sometimes," Isabelle said, trotting a few steps with the gelding.

"Dismount immediately! You don't trot a limping horse that way!"

Leonard seemed to have lost his patience altogether and Isabelle must have been scared by his outburst because she didn't protest again, but dismounted Red Top, who stood still with his right foreleg lifted a little, his head hanging and his ears straight out.

Leonard squeezed and felt Red Top's leg. He muttered to himself and when Isabelle's dad came down into the ring, he shook his head.

"It looks like he's got a sprain. You'd better take him home and call the vet right away."

"Vet? What for? He'll rest for a week or so and then he'll be fine," Gruenwald said, taking Red Top's reins and leading the horse toward the gate.

Isabelle plodded behind with her nose in the air and her

crop flippantly swinging and slapping her boot. Lori made an angry face at her back.

When the Gruenwalds had disappeared to take Red Top to the horse trailer and go home, Leonard sighed deeply before commanding the remaining riders into trot. They had to exercise a little again to get warm in the cold indoor riding ring and get the horses up to speed.

The rest of the lesson went without a hitch, and when it was over Lori made Tony jump really nicely a couple of times. She gave him lots of praise and happily stroked his neck. Kate and Kariba did well, too. The chestnut mare jumped at least as well as, if not better than, the bigger and more experienced half-breeds in the group.

Kate shone like the sun when Leonard praised her and Kariba. Lori smiled happily. She was glad that at least Kate did well, since she and Tony weren't that great.

On the way home the two girls walked their horses together and discussed how they could make Isabelle sell Red Top to Lori without it being too expensive.

There were so many problems. First of all, James Gruenwald would certainly demand as much for Red Top now as he'd paid for the horse. Also, Lori didn't know if her parents would agree to buy such a mistreated horse, and she didn't think they'd ever let her buy him if they had known how he'd performed in class today.

The third and probably worst problem was that Isabelle

would never sell Red Top to Lori, not since Lori got to instruct the quadrille when Isabelle had wanted to.

Lori groaned when she considered all these problems. She absently stroked Tony's neck, but he shook his head. He was on his way home, and he wanted to get there as quickly as possible.

Chapter 9

"Listen up," Kate said, reading aloud from a horse magazine with a lot of horse ads. *"Well ridden mare, five years old, 62 inches, after Feliciano…* The area code is ours. I think you should call them."

Lori nodded and also read aloud, *"Gelding, good jumper, four years old, pedigree unknown, chestnut, phone…"*

"That one sounds good too," Kate said. "Come on, let's make some calls."

The girls had dedicated Sunday morning to finding horses in the ads. There were lots of horses to choose from and Lori was optimistic when she sat down by the phone to make the first call of the day.

Her stomach tingled when she thought that maybe one of the horses that they had circled might some day be her own.

Several of them were ponies, since Lori thought it would be easier to find a pony for three thousand dollars than a big horse, but she still hoped to find a half-breed as big as Kariba, who was 61 inches at the withers.

She first called about the mare after Feliciano, but it was already sold. The gelding that liked jumping was still for sale, but his owners wanted five thousand dollars for him.

"He's a real find," the voice in the phone told Lori. "A real find for anybody who wants a horse with real fire in him."

Lori sighed when she hung up. The two first calls hadn't turned out very well.

"So call about this one," Kate suggested and read, *"Beautiful New Forest Pony, 58 inches, has done A Jumping and easy dressage."*

"I'm sure it's too expensive," Lori sighed.

She dialed the number anyway. She was right, the pony was six thousand dollars plus tax and the girl wanted to sell it to a competition rider.

Lori hung up. This was going really badly.

"Crossbreed pony, 57 inches, ridden and jumped, low price to the right home…"

Kate almost jumped up and down on her chair when she read the ad.

"That line about *low price to the right home* sounded nice," Lori said and quickly dialed the number.

The number was busy and she waited for five minutes before calling again.

Lori scheduled about two hours to go to see three horses that sounded good and that she and her parents were welcome to take a look at. The horses were a dark brown pony gelding, a retired trotter and a crossbreed without papers but supposedly a very good jumper.

After talking to Leonard and her parents she called the three sellers again and asked if it was okay to come on the following Wednesday. They had the day off from school, and since the horses at the riding school were resting on Wednesdays Leonard didn't mind coming along and taking a look at the horses Lori had chosen.

All the sellers agreed to that and Lori was satisfied when she hung up after her last call. She was finally doing what she had dreamed of for so long – finding her own horse to take care of and love!

Lori thought Wednesday would never come, but suddenly one morning her alarm clock woke her and she realized that today was *the* day with a big D.

Lori, her mother and Kate were scheduled to pick Leonard up at the riding school at nine to go and look at the first horse. This was the retired trotter, who was on a farm less than six miles from town.

Lori sat chewing her nails nervously all the way, and she

thought they'd never get there. Leonard mostly sat quietly and Lori's mother concentrated on driving. Kate tried to talk and keep the conversation going, but it was hard because Lori hardly answered her.

The farm where the trotter was stabled seemed totally deserted, and without knowing what they were supposed to do the four walked into a little building they thought was the stable.

It actually was the stable, but it was dark and dirty and smelled pungently of horse dung and ammonia. There were a couple of horses in stalls. One was a ragged Draft horse that looked black in the weak light and the other was a long-legged, thin, light brown horse with long ears and a narrow, thin neck.

Leonard muttered a little. He didn't seem to like the horse and Lori looked at her mother and Kate.

At that moment, the back door of the dark stable opened and a short fat man with sideburns came up to them. He introduced himself as Mr. Brown and he was the owner of Fay To Trot, as the trotter was called.

Mr. Brown spoke warmly of the horse for a couple of minutes while Leonard silently investigated the horse's legs and teeth.

Lori asked to try riding him and Mr. Brown said he would see to it at once. He disappeared and came back after a while, carrying a ragged saddle and an old worn bridle with a rusty bit.

"Now don't expect too much," he said, smiling at Lori. "The old guy hasn't been ridden very much since my daughter started high school this fall. That's why we're selling him. She doesn't have the time."

Lori saddled and bridled the horse herself without problems. Then she led the gelding out from the stable and adjusted the leathers.

The horse looked terrible in the sharp September sun. He was thin and wretched and seemed totally listless.

Lori tried riding for a short while in a pen behind the stable, but she already knew that she didn't want this horse. No wonder he was cheap. He was hardly worth even the few thousand the old man was asking for him.

Lori dismounted with disappointment and thanked him for the visit, and then everybody got in the car again and went to see the next horse.

"One horse that should be slaughtered," Leonard snorted, and Lori's mother nodded in agreement.

"I felt sorry for him," Kate said. "I'm sure he'd be all right if some nice person took care of him and fed him and…"

"Well, he might get fat, but he'd hardly be all right. He was thick from gall in all four legs and he had splints on both forelegs," Leonard said.

Lori sighed. It was a good thing that Leonard was with them. She hadn't seen either the galls or the splints.

The next horse they went to see was the pony gelding, and Lori's mother drove straight there. The place was about twelve miles from the first stable and Lori started feeling nervous again. Maybe this would be her dream horse?

The pony was in a private stable out in the country, and when they got there a big heavy girl was sitting on a bench outside, waiting for them.

"So, you're the ones who want to see Morocco. He's in the stable right now."

Lori, Kate, Rita and Leonard followed the girl into a nice, well-lit stable. In a clean stall stood a pony that apparently was Morocco. Lori immediately fell for him. He had a cute pony face and a wonderfully round, nice body. He was about 57 inches, and Lori was sure she'd found a good horse.

Without saying anything the girl went to get the saddle and bridle. While she was away, Leonard took a careful look at the pony gelding.

"Well, he seems to be all right," he said and smiled at Lori, who nodded happily.

Once again, she got to saddle and bridle the horse herself, and the girl who owned Morocco showed the way to a riding ring where Lori could try the horse out.

"He can be a little silly when you mount him," the girl said, helping Lori adjust the leathers. "You'd better watch out, so he doesn't run away with you before you're ready."

"What do you men, 'run away'?" Leonard asked in a harsh voice.

"He has some bad habits that I haven't been able to stop. One of them is that he sometimes gallops as soon as you're up on his back," the girl said, turning to Leonard who just shook his head.

Lori put her foot in the stirrup and the next moment the horse careened away. The girl who owned him tried in vain to get hold of his reins but missed them, and before Lori had her foot in the other stirrup the horse had bucked and thrown her to the ground.

The world spun for a moment before Lori carefully got to her feet and tried to feel if anything was broken. Morocco was a bit further off, making friends with a horse in the pen next to the riding course.

Leonard looked grim.

"No thank you, I don't think this horse is for Lori," Rita said in a worried voice and shook her blonde head.

"But he never does it more than once," the girl said, trying to get hold of the pony who merrily jumped away as soon as she got close to him.

"You are quite right, Rita," Leonard said, "this isn't the right horse for us. Thanks for letting us see him. Come on, let's go to the next place."

Lori was disappointed when they left the private stable and the temperamental pony.

"Well," Lori's mom sighed, "we only have one horse left, but we don't have to be there until twelve and it's only ten thirty. How about some coffee in that shop?"

Leonard thought that was a great idea. He never said no to coffee, and Lori and Kate didn't mind getting ice cream.

While they were at the coffee shop they kept talking about horses, and Leonard gave them a lesson in what to consider when they were checking out a horse.

The most important thing was that the horse's general condition be good, and that the horse was shining and well fed.

It was also important to look at how the horse acted as you examined it, and the legs were very important. They had to be dry and firm, without galls or splints.

Lori and Kate listened attentively. This really was good stuff to know.

When they got in the car again and drove toward the next horse, Lori was in a much better mood. She was sure this horse would be fine. According to the girl she had spoken to on the phone it was a cross between a Thoroughbred and a Fjord horse, cream-colored and 60 inches high. It had been ridden and jumped a few times.

Lori sat dreaming about the horse all through the trip. She would care so well for him, train him carefully and maybe do competitions after a while. At least club competitions at the riding school.

Rita drove onto a long dirt road. They seemed to be at

the right place, since two small fat ponies were grazing in a pen next to the road. Lori wondered where the horse they were here to see could be.

They had hardly stopped when a little bird-like lady and a tall girl with glasses and blonde hair came out of a yellow house and walked toward them. When they'd said hi they were shown into the stable. It seemed to be an old rebuilt barn, since it smelled more of cows than of horses. In a calf pen in a corner was a fat horse of some anonymous gray or yellow color. The legs were like matches, the neck was short and fat and the horse's hind legs were too tall.

"This is Golden Boy," as we call him, the bird-like lady said and proudly indicated the horse with her hand.

"How old is he?" Leonard asked.

"He's two and a half, but he's already been both ridden and jumped and we've also been driving him," the lady said proudly.

Leonard knitted his prominent eyebrows and looked angry.

"Do you mean that you've been breaking in a two-year old, and even jumping him?" he said with a voice that was so harsh that the lady gave him a surprised look.

"Yes, of course, with Thoroughbreds you should start when they're two. Isn't that right?"

"But this isn't a Thoroughbred," Leonard said, staring at the lady who had to look down.

"Well, no, there's that… But he has a lot of Thoroughbred

in him, if I may say. It's true that the mother is a Fjord horse, but the father is a genuine Thoroughbred trotter."

"Thoroughbred trotter! You mean an ordinary trotter?"

The lady started to shy back, since Leonard's cross-examination wasn't very friendly, and Lori was a little ashamed of him. She knew that he was strongly opposed to breaking young horses in too early, but she had no idea that he could act this way toward anyone.

On the other hand, she felt that he was doing the right thing. The old lady and her daughter might have ruined this horse for life out of pure lack of knowledge.

"Yes, his father is a trotter."

It was the first thing the tall girl had said, and Leonard turned to her.

"You don't have to get the saddle and bridle, because we will absolutely not be buying this horse," Leonard said firmly and marched out of the stable.

Lori, Rita and Kate thanked the lady quietly with a look and then went out of the stable after him. Leonard was already in the front seat of the car, his face red with anger. Rita had hardly started the car before he started lecturing about damages to the back, muscles and other nasty things that could occur from breaking horses in too early. Lori and Kate nodded and agreed. They both felt it was totally wrong to break a horse in that early. The best thing was to wait until the horse was four.

"Well, this wasn't very fun," Leonard said when the car drove up to the riding school again, "but keep looking and I'm sure you'll find a good horse. Too bad that I sold that chestnut before I knew you were looking for a horse of your own."

Lori's heart jumped into her mouth. Had she been that close to buying her dream horse?

"Chestnut?" Rita looked at Leonard. "What horse is that?"

"A horse I sold to the wrong person," Leonard said and shrugged his heavy shoulders. "I regret it now, because the girl who bought him really can't handle him."

"And there's no chance of buying him?" Rita asked.

Lori held her breath, but Leonard shook his gray head and sighed, "Unfortunately I don't think so. We'll see in a while. Well, home again. Bye for now!"

Leonard jumped out of the car and waved to Rita, Lori and Kate as they left the yard in front of the riding school and drove off down the road.

"Too bad about Red Top," Kate quietly said to Lori.

Lori nodded. She knew that this would nag at her for the rest of her life, that she had been that close to buying her dream horse. It was enough to make her cry!

Chapter 10

That evening Lori's group practiced the quadrille again, so Lori took the bus to the riding school. She was dead on her feet after the busy day. First she had looked at the three horses, then she and Kate had taken a long ride in the woods, and now she was on her way to the riding school. She knew that the practice would last at least an hour and a half.

The Horse Day was quickly getting closer and the quadrille show still wasn't quite ingrained in the eight girls and their horses. Every now and then somebody rode the wrong way or missed something, and then they had to start all over again.

Lori knew that Isabelle still wanted to take over the quadrille exercise, since she thought she could do it better than Lori.

Many of the younger girls in the stable looked up to Isabelle. Lori had heard that Isabelle had started what amounted to a hate campaign against Lori after Isabelle and her parents hadn't been able to persuade Leonard that Isabelle should lead the quadrille exercise.

Lori really didn't care about this. She wasn't spending that much time at the riding school now, and if people liked talking about her behind her back, they were welcome to. It was worse that Isabelle had a few admirers among the girls in the quadrille.

Strangely, it was almost always one of these three who ruined the program for the others, and sometimes Lori quietly wondered if they were doing it on purpose. Most often it was Lisa on the Welsh pony Pluto, Hanna on Linette and Linda on Klara who made trouble.

The strange thing was that they all were riding in the two last pairs and should understand that they only had to follow the horses in front of them. But still they rode left instead of right and did other things backwards, as if they were riding the program for the first time.

Lori was actually worried about them. She was afraid that they were going to make a fool of her on Horse Day by riding the wrong way and then saying that Lori hadn't trained the group properly.

The riding school stable was silent and empty, and Lori suspected that the eight quadrille riders were already in the ring, being warmed up by Leonard. She could hear marching music from the speakers, and with firm steps Lori walked toward the ring.

Halfway through the passageway that connected the stable to the ring she met James Gruenwald, who gave her a haughty look.

"You don't have to be there today," he said, standing in Lori's way.

Lori raised her eyebrows in surprise.

"Isabelle has already taken over the group, and she's doing great. I've heard that you had some problems with them so Leonard let Isabelle try, and it's working fine. It's actually working great."

Lori quickly stepped aside and passed Gruenwald. She could verify that he'd told the truth soon enough. Isabelle was standing in the middle of the ring, snapping her crop and ordering the group around. Lisa, Hanna and Linda were looking strangely satisfied, and of course they always rode in the right direction.

Lori cleared her throat and opened the gate to the ring. She quickly walked up to Isabelle, who was standing with her back to her and still hadn't seen that Lori was closing in.

"May I ask what you're doing?" Lori said coldly to Isabelle, who quickly spun around and gave Lori a murderous look.

"I've taken over here," Isabelle said with a voice that was as haughty as her father's, sticking her nose in the air.

"Really?" Lori said. "How strange that nobody told me."

Lori's face was rigid with anger, and she really had to control herself to keep calm and not hit Isabelle, who was standing looking proud with a silly smile on her face.

"There you are, Lori!"

Leonard came down into the ring and gave Lori an apologetic smile. She didn't understand a thing. Leonard was making a fuss over Isabelle, that much was clear. Lori angrily looked at Leonard's smiling face.

She clenched her jaws together to avoid saying something stupid, and with her face white from anger she turned around to leave the ring. She heard Leonard saying something to Isabelle, and then he followed her.

He caught up with her in the clubroom and amicably asked her to come into his office for a while. Lori's face looked ready to explode with anger. She didn't want to stay another moment. She felt that he had let her down.

"I understand that you're sad and angry, Lori, but Marianne and I have terrible problems with our finances right now," Leonard said, sitting down on the chair behind his desk.

Lori sat down across from him. She could feel her anger slowly ebbing away and being replaced by a very bad conscience.

Leonard leaned back and went on, "As you may know, we've applied for state funding this year, but we're still not sure if they'll give us any. If they do it'll be great, but if not we don't even know if the riding school can survive the winter. We may have to close down."

Lori blushed and looked at her hands. She was beginning to understand how James Gruenwald had been able to persuade Leonard to make Isabelle the leader of the quadrille in Lori's place, and she was ashamed for thinking that Leonard had let her down.

"For now, Marianne and I have taken a bank loan of fifteen thousand dollars, and we hope that that will cover our debts up till Christmas. The guarantor for the loan is James Gruenwald and his company. He's also promised to sponsor the riding club with fifteen thousand dollars if we advertise for him in the indoor riding ring and on our big truck."

"I see…" Lori said and looked up. "I'm sorry for getting so mad before…"

"I understand you completely," Leonard said and smiled at her. "You've been working very hard with the quadrille, and you've also done other things for the riding club. It's too bad that this has to happen."

At that moment, the door to the office opened and Gruenwald and Isabelle walked in. They both looked triumphant and Isabelle was smiling venomously.

"Well now," Gruenwald panted, looking angry, "so that's how it is! My little Isabelle isn't good enough and you're just fawning to get my money."

Isabelle looked haughty. "Well, Leonard, I really didn't think you were this type of person. I'll be leaving this club right away."

"What's this supposed to mean?" Lori said, getting up from her chair. She was almost too angry to speak.

It was clear that Mr. Gruenwald and Isabelle had been listening at the door for some time, hearing every word that Lori and Leonard had said. Lori was so mad that she didn't really know what to do. She stared into Mr. Gruenwald's eyes and growled, "So, you've been listening at the door? Aren't you ashamed? That's so low!"

"Look who's talking!" Isabelle shouted in a shrill voice. "You, sitting here and back-stabbing me with Leonard!"

"I haven't said one bad word about you, but I'm going to now," Lori roared and took one step toward Isabelle, who shied back in fright.

"You come here and think that you're so great, you're snobbish and act as if you own the entire world. But let me tell you that you don't. You've managed to get Lisa, Linda and Hanna to obey you and destroy every exercise I've had with the quadrille group! You've been spreading so many rumors about me with the others here at the riding school that at least half of my friends have come to me and asked if you're in your right mind, thanks to the fairy tales you've been making up about me!"

"I have not!" Isabelle screamed, white faced with rage.

"Lori, calm down, please!"

Leonard stood up behind his desk and looked as if he wanted to intervene, but there was no stopping Lori.

"But all of this," Lori went on in a threateningly quiet and calm voice, "is nothing compared to the worst thing you've done."

"And what's that?" Isabelle said, regaining her self-assurance for a moment.

"You've ruined a good horse, a dream horse, a wonderful riding horse that could have become great. You've been beating him, and you've destroyed his mouth…"

"I have not! You're lying! Dad, tell her she's lying!"

"Shut up!" Lori roared.

She took one step more and came up just in front of Isabelle, who was standing with her back to the doorframe.

"I'm not lying," she continued. "One of my best friends was in your stable, and she knows exactly how you've been treating Red Top. She told me that you hardly give him any oats, that you always ride with running reins and that you don't dare lead him into the stable yourself, because he kicks you out of the stall."

Lori fell silent and drew a breath. She was close to tears from anger and rage. At last, she had gotten to tell Isabelle all the things that had been nagging her.

She thought gratefully of her friend Tanja, who had been nice and followed another girl to Isabelle's stable for a couple of days, helping out with another pony that was stabled there. While she was there, she had witnessed firsthand how Red Top was treated.

"Dad! Let's leave!"

Isabelle turned on her heel and disappeared out the door.

"Well, Swanson, don't count on any more loans in my name, you'd better believe that!"

"And I'm calling the paper," Lori said angrily. "Don't think that you're getting out of this without losing every customer you've had here at the riding school, and *you'd* better believe *that!*"

James Gruenwald just snorted and then followed Isabelle, disappearing through the door.

Leonard sat down again, hiding his face in his hands. Lori looked at him.

"Well, that's that," he sighed. "I guess we can say goodbye to the riding school now, Lori. I'll go bankrupt."

Lori turned cold with fear. What had she done now? Bankrupt!

"I'm calling Kate's dad," she said firmly. "He's a reporter at the paper. I'm sure they'll write about it."

"And what good will that do?"

"It may not help us, but if it means trouble for Gruenwald's chain of stores I, for one, will be very happy," Lori said, dialing the number.

"Hello, Green residence."

"Hi, it's Lori."

"Hi," Kate's dad said, "and I gather you want to speak to Kate?"

"No, I would actually like to talk to you. You see…"

Lori told him everything, and Kate's dad was upset. Things like this weren't acceptable in a club that was funded by the state.

"The state?" Lori said sadly. "No, I doubt we'll be getting any funds."

Then she fell silent for a long while, listening attentively before she happily put her hand over the receiver and yelled to Leonard, "We got it! The funding! More than thirty five thousand dollars!"

Leonard looked up. He couldn't believe his ears.

"Give me the phone, honey. Yes, this is Leonard Swanson here. What are you saying? We got the funding? How much? You were at the meeting today?"

He fell silent, and Lori danced a wild dance across the office floor. A few of the quadrille girls came in, and they looked questioningly at Lori, who tried to explain what had happened in whispers.

When they understood they all started jumping around and hugging each other and Lori, and when Leonard finally hung up he leapt from his chair.

"This is crazy, Lori! Thanks for your help! Thirty five thousand! This calls for a celebration!"

Chapter 11

Suddenly, there were only three days to go to the Horse
Day. Lori was surprised when she realized that a month
and a half had already gone by since the meeting in the
clubroom that day.

The girls had spent the two last weeks painting fences
and poles, making prizes for the raffles, getting officials
for the competitions on Sunday and preparing a lot of
other stuff. The mood in the stable, where more and more
riders had begun helping out with the Horse Day, was quite
different now. Every night Lori fell asleep as soon as she
laid her head on her pillow, and she could hardly wake up
when the alarm went off each morning.

Everything was so much fun and there were so many
things going on at once that if she hadn't known that Red

Top was still in Isabelle's stable, she'd have been totally happy.

The fact that she knew that Isabelle was treating Red Top badly, that he didn't get the food he needed and that she was riding him although he may be lame, was hanging over her like a dark cloud and making everything else seem a little duller.

Kate, Madeline and Emma tried to cheer her up as much as they could, but now that there were only three days left before the show, Lori was getting sadder and more subdued by the minute.

Lori was on the competition committee with Maria Idelson, the club secretary, and had been helping her sort the entries for Sunday's jumping competitions. She knew that Red Top and Isabelle were signed up for both jumping competitions for big horses on Sunday afternoon.

Today was Wednesday, and Lori started school a little later than usual. For once, the newspaper arrived before she went to school, and she quickly leafed through it. It wasn't until she came to the ads that she jumped.

Crossbred gelding, golden chestnut, after Jimmy Ripkin, to be sold to highest bidder, temperamental competition horse with nice walks and a future in both jumping and dressage.

Lori quickly ran into the hall and grabbed the phone book.

Yes, it really was the Gruenwald's phone number! Red Top was being sold? To the highest bidder? I wonder how much he'll go for, Lori thought as she went into the kitchen to have breakfast.

"Any good news in the paper today?" Rita asked, yawning as she came into the kitchen in her bathrobe.

"There's an ad for Red Top, that horse that Leonard thought we should buy."

"Let me have a look. But how do you know this is Red Top?"

"Everything fits. And that's the Gruenwald's number. I checked it out."

"How much do you think they want for him? And how is that horse, really?"

"You and Dad will be there on Sunday. You'll see him then, because he'll be in both jumping competitions for big horses."

"Is he a good jumper?"

"Well, not now, really. Isabelle has totally ruined him."

Lori sighed. Suddenly it felt as if Sunday was an eternity away. Just imagine if she were able to buy Red Top after all!

But there was still a risk that Lori would never be able to afford him anyway…

In the afternoon, there was a dress rehearsal at the riding school, and everybody who had something to do with the Horse Day was there. Besides leading the quadrille, Lori was riding in something called "The Horse Through the Ages."

This was a number where all kinds of horses could participate and where every rider had to wear a costume.

Lori had talked George into letting her borrow Tony as a circus horse. She planned to dress as a clown in red and white tights that her mother had sewn, a funny pointed hat with red dots and a big red false nose that she had bought in a toy store.

She wasn't sure that Tony would recognize her when he saw her.

Tony was going to have a lot of red feathers in his bridle. He was lightly reined and Lori had borrowed a lunging rein from George with side reins attached. Also, Lori had a couple of red reins that her mother had sewn, and Kate had helped her learn to stand on Tony's back when he was walking.

It wasn't really that hard, but it did feel a little scary and Lori wasn't sure that she'd dare do it in front of an audience. Suppose Tony got scared and took off? She'd fall off in half a second!

In the costume show there were, among others, a cowboy, an Indian girl, a girl dressed as a medieval knight, and in a little trolley pulled by Vicki, the stable's Shetland pony, was a little girl wearing a long dress with a cute little hat on her head.

Leonard had a buddy who was breeding Belgian Drafts and who had let him borrow a beautiful dark brown gelding named Tough. Tough was to pull a harrow and walk at the end of the procession. Later, he would even out the sand in the ring every now and then to make it look nice and tidy.

Of course, there were lots of other acts. Marianne would show advanced dressage on the half-breed Bianca, and there was to be a jumping competition with the most advanced pony riders and senior riders. There would be lunging and vaulting among the many events and, as the finishing touch, the pony quadrille would come in for the big finale.

After Lori's quarrel with Isabelle everything had worked out better. Lori had told a few of the girls in the group that she knew that they had wanted Isabelle as their coach, but from now on it was she, Lori, who would coach them. If this wasn't to their liking, they should quit right away so she would have the time to find replacements for them.

The dress rehearsal worked fine and Lori felt so sure on Tony's back that she actually tried standing up on his back. Leonard was impressed and said that he himself wouldn't dare trying that, even on Vicki.

Lori tried to imagine Leonard standing on Vicki's back, but she had to shake her head. It was just impossible.

When the dress rehearsal was done, Leonard and Marianne invited everyone to a celebration with juice and cinnamon buns in the clubroom. The room quickly filled with hungry riders and the mood was lively.

Lori was sitting with Kate, Madeline and some others, discussing whether ponies or big horses made better jumpers.

Lori enjoyed sitting with her friends and feeling that she was one of them. The mood at the riding school was much better since Isabelle had left.

Suddenly there was a noise from the stable and the girl who was closest to the door got up to see what was happening. She soon came back and called out that the skewbald was loose.

Lori quickly got to her feet and hurried out. Tony was a master at crawling out of his head-collar, and she wasn't sure that she'd checked it properly.

Tony was walking through the big passageway in the middle of the stable quickly and Lori hurried to catch up to him. When he saw her coming, he just as quickly turned around and went in the other direction, disappearing to the left, into one of the narrow side corridors.

"Get him from that direction!" Lori called to the others.

The girl who was with her took a few fast steps in that direction. Lori could just make out Tony behind the rows of stalls, and she could see that the horses in the stalls were irritated with him. Several of them were kicking as the gelding walked by.

Lori was scared to death that one of them might hit him. Why hadn't she checked that he was properly tied up? She was usually so careful.

The girl was just grabbing for Tony's mane when he realized that he was on the verge of being caught. He clumsily pushed by her and came out into the big passageway again.

Lori carefully walked toward him, but he quickly turned around again. This time Tony slipped on the smooth cement floor, and when he walked away Lori could see that he was limping a little on one foreleg.

Finally, the other girl managed to grab Tony's bangs, and Lori gratefully walked up to them.

"Thanks a lot!" she said, smiling.

"Not at all," the girl said cheerfully.

Lori led Tony over to the stall she had borrowed for him. He was clearly limping on the right foreleg. Lori looked at him, worried. Would he go lame now, three days before Horse Day and four days before their first competition?

Lori carefully examined the leg. It was warm and had already started swelling down at the fetlock. Lori bit her lip.

"Darn it," she muttered. "I'll have to get Leonard."

Lori quickly went back to the clubroom, which was emptying now. She got Leonard, who was sitting and talking to Marianne and a couple of the private owners. He immediately came with her, and all the way over to Tony's stall Lori hoped and prayed that the gelding's leg would have gotten better again.

Leonard stroked and squeezed, and then stood up and sighed.

"He's sprained his leg badly. Look, the joint's already swollen."

Lori nodded and asked what she should do.

"Well, there really isn't much to do. You'll have to let him rest until he's healed again. I guess I'll have to drive him home in the horse trailer."

"Thanks," Lori said, feeling a lot better, "That would be great. Should I call a vet?"

"Yeah, I guess that would be best."

Leonard stroked his chin and looked thoughtful.

"Call that new vet," he said, "They says she's good. She's supposed to take over from the old local veterinarian next spring."

It was a good thing that it was easy to get Tony into horse trailers, Lori thought as she was sitting up front in the truck on their way to Lind Farm a while later. She had just walked in and Tony had followed her like a well-trained dog.

When they arrived at Lind Farm, George immediately came out and asked why Tony was coming home in a transport. Lori explained what had happened and George shook his head, sighing, "And you were to be in that competition. That's really too bad."

Lori also sighed and helped Leonard unload Tony, who obediently let himself be led into the stall where a big armful of hay was waiting for him.

George and Lori thanked Leonard for his help, and just moments after he'd left Kate appeared on the forest road with Kariba, who neighed eagerly when she saw that they were home.

"I'll call the vet tomorrow morning," Lori offered.

George nodded. "You do that. She can come by anytime. I'll be home all day."

"I guess I'll be coming here too," Lori said morosely.

"But what about school?"

"Oh right, school." Lori shrugged her shoulders. "I'm so distracted I hardly care about school right now, but I'll arrange for her to come after."

"A typical strained muscle," the young vet said, patting Tony's neck.

"Is it bad?" Lori asked, but the vet shook her head and smiled reassuringly.

"No, but he'll have to take it easy for two weeks. You absolutely can't ride him. But you can lead him around for a short time every day."

"Can he walk in the pen during the day?"

"Yeah, I guess that'll be all right. By the way, do you know how to put on a cold sterile dressing?"

Lori nodded. She had learned that at a course about caring for sick horses last spring.

"Do that every day if you can. That should reduce the swelling," the vet said.

Lori led Tony to the pen while the vet put her stuff back into the car and wrote a receipt for Lori, who paid her. Then she said goodbye and drove away.

Lori slowly walked back to the pen.

The sun was shining from a clear blue October sky and everything was unbelievably beautiful with all the red and yellow leaves blazing like fire against the sky. But Lori, leaning tiredly against the gate and watching the grazing horses, couldn't see that.

"Typical," she said straight into the air. "I've been training and working this horse for a month and a half, and now, when all the training's finally paid off, he goes lame!"

Lori sighed and went back to the yard where her mother was just pulling up with the car to pick her up.

Chapter 12

The Horse Day had finally come, and Lori awoke before the alarm went off and rubbed the sleep out of her eyes.

The pony quadrille was the first thought in her head. Then her thoughts went to her clown costume and the horse she was to ride in "The Horse Through the Ages."

She had been allowed to borrow one of the riding school's private ponies, also a skewbald, but black and white and just 51 inches high. Lori wasn't very heavy and would easily be able to ride Popcorn, although she was a little too tall.

She got up and went into the bathroom for a quick morning shower before breakfast. It didn't feel like the Horse Day at all, she thought, but just like an ordinary Saturday, except that she was up unusually early. It was only five thirty, and Kate and her mother wouldn't come to pick her up until seven.

Of course the alarm went off while Lori was in the shower, and she could hear her mother get out of bed to turn it off. Lori felt a little guilty. She hadn't intended to wake her mother up.

The newspaper fell through the mail slot with a thud, and when she went to the kitchen Lori picked it up and had a look. She found the usual stuff about club meetings and sports, and lots of advertisements.

If it weren't for the ads, her parents would never subscribe to the paper, Lori suspected.

Outside the kitchen window it was dark and cold, and the streetlights were faint. Her window was almost the only one lit, and Lori wondered if Emma had gotten up yet.

Emma lived two floors above Lori in the same apartment, and was also going with Kate's mom at seven.

"It would be typical of Emma to oversleep," Lori muttered and started heating milk for her cocoa.

At five to seven she was ready. Heavily dressed and with a big bag filled with her clown costume, a lunch and a thermos of cocoa, she walked down the stairs and into the street where Kate and her mom were already waiting. Emma came down a minute later and Lori asked if she had overslept.

"How did you know?" Emma said with surprise. "I woke up at quarter to seven."

Lori laughed and said that she'd just guessed.

At the riding school, people were already gathering in the clubroom. Everybody was waiting for Leonard to come and tell them what to do. He was feeding the riding school horses, and there was an unbelievable noise as the horses neighed and kicked their stall walls. Lori went to sit at a table with Emma, Madeline and Kate.

"Good morning," Leonard said a little later when he entered the clubroom.

He sat down at one of the tables and took a sheet of paper from his pocket. On the paper he had written everybody's tasks. Lori hoped that she wouldn't have to do anything besides ride in "The Horse Through the Ages" and worry about the pony quadrille, but she soon found out that she also had to sell tickets before the show.

Furthermore, she was to lead the pony Pluto during the pony ride and afterwards. Lori sighed. Yes, horses were a lot of fun, but they also meant a lot of work, and at the moment she mostly longed for a warm bed and a soft pillow.

Lori felt a little better when she had started working. First of all, every horse in the stable had to be brushed and groomed while Leonard and the stable girl Jasmine mucked out and cleaned everything.

Lori started by grooming little Popcorn and then went on to one of the big riding school horses, the skewbald Gordon.

Gordon wasn't easy to clean. Like most horses he loved

to get dirty, and Lori had to work hard to get him shining and light gray instead of dirty yellow. She finally had to give up, but at least he looked a tiny bit cleaner.

There were lots of things that had to be done, and Lori continued by helping one of the younger girls braid the pony Jock, who would also be in "The Horse Through the Ages."

Lori thought seriously about braiding Popcorn too, but when she got to his stall Popcorn's owner Robin was already there. Matt, who was ten years old, had said that he wasn't the least bit interested in the Horse Day. Now he seemed to have changed his mind, and he looked a little embarrassed when he saw Lori.

"Is it all right if I come along too? I can walk beside you. My mom made a clown costume for me."

"Of course you can," Lori said, smiling at him. "But wouldn't it be better if you ride? After all, I'm a little too big for Popcorn."

Matt nodded happily and kept on braiding his pony. Lori walked toward Leonard, who was just cleaning the stalls. He gave her the shovel that Jasmine had used earlier and asked her to help him. It was nice to see how neat all the stalls looked with new, clean bedding.

One could feel the mood rising, and most people were getting nervous. Joanna, who was going to ride her newly broken in young horse Diamond, was bustling about and making everybody feel stressed out.

The two best dressage riders in the club, Josie and Anna, were going to ride a difficult dressage program, mirroring each other, and now they were standing together, going through the program over and over again. Lori smiled at them. It was a little hard to ride a dressage program without the horses.

Down by the otherwise empty sick stall, Catherine was grooming her competition pony, Blackie. She and the best senior rider in the club, Evan who rode Mistral, were working together on their duel jump.

Catherine didn't seem very nervous, but then she had jumped in the local championships during the summer. Evan and Mistral had also qualified well, but not as well as Catherine and Blackie.

In almost every horse stall there were kids grooming, braiding unruly pony manes, or oiling hooves. Everybody was nicely dressed in clean jodhpurs and Leonard had suggested that everyone who had a club sweater with the club logo should wear it.

Leonard got the borrowed Belgian Draft gelding and raked the riding course with the harrow one last time. Two of the younger students made white sawdust markings in front of the letters on the course that showed the different moves in the dressage programs, and soon it was time for the officials to go to their stations.

Lori sighed and went to the box office by the door.

When she peered out, she could see that there were already cars driving into the parking lot by the riding school.

Her stomach fluttered a little. In spite of the state funding, this day was important for the future of the riding school.

Leonard had spoken to the paper, and with luck somebody would also come from the local radio station. Several of the people on the state executive board had kids riding at the school and would hopefully come to look and be impressed enough to give money to the school again next year, maybe even more money.

More and more cars came up the road, and it was getting close to ten o'clock, when everything was scheduled to begin.

Lori drew a deep breath when she sold her first ticket to an elderly lady.

The Horse Day had begun!

Chapter 13

Lori hadn't needed to worry about people coming. The indoor riding ring was almost bursting when everybody finally took their places in the stands. Lori counted her ticket stubs. She discovered that she'd sold more than four hundred and fifty tickets!

Finally, when Karl Fenton greeted everybody over the loudspeaker system, Lori was relieved of her box office duties by Maria Idelson, and quickly ran off to change into her clown costume.

She heard Karl Fenton announce the first act of the day, the mirror riding with Josie and Anna. Lori was a little sad that she wouldn't get to see it.

The clubroom had been reworked into a coffee shop and was empty at the moment, but in the big room that had once been the clubroom there were lots of girls changing clothes.

There wasn't too much space and the air was hot and humid, but everybody was in high spirits and seemed to be having fun. Lori made her way into the corner where she'd put her bag earlier in the morning, next to Kate's and Emma's.

Strange! Somebody must have opened the bag. Lori was totally sure that she remembered closing the zipper again after checking that the thermos wasn't leaking.

Lori shook her head. This was strange. Who could have done it? She'd probably forgotten to close the bag after all.

"Who's in now?" Eva asked.

Eva was sitting in gym clothes, waiting for her turn. Eva and another girl were going to ride vaults on the Fjord horse Fjodor, but although the program was difficult none of the girls seemed nervous.

"I think they're riding the young horses now," Emma said, pulling her black riding jacket on.

"We'd better go down then. Come on, Eva," the other girl said and they went down the stairs together.

Lori sat down on the rickety bench and took her lunch out of the bag. She carefully put it down on the floor and then pulled out her clown costume.

It looks strange, she thought to herself. Wrinkled! Lori remembered how carefully she'd folded it and put it in the bag in the morning, to be sure it would look nice.

"Oh, no!"

Lori's outcry made all the other girls fall silent and turn to her. Lori was holding her clown costume up in front of her. It was full of big holes and torn in several places. With tears in her eyes Lori looked at what had been a cute clown costume in red and white earlier the same morning, but now was just shreds of torn fabric.

"Who did this?" Kate screamed, looking around.

"That's so rotten!" Emma exclaimed.

"I can't believe anyone here would ruin your costume like that," Madeline said in both anger and surprise, and most of the girls agreed.

Lori sank to the bench behind her. She was close to tears.

"But why! I can't understand it!" Kate said, putting her arm around Lori's shoulders.

"No, it's so terrible!" Emma agreed.

Then she gave all the other girls a hard look.

"Have any of you seen or heard anything?"

"Well, not that I want to tell tales," a blonde, shorthaired girl with freckles said, "but I've heard that Lori and Isabelle aren't friends. Couldn't it be one of Isabelle's friends?"

"It would be typical for Isabelle to come up with something like that," Kate nodded, getting up from the bench. "What should we do?"

"I'll have to skip the procession," Lori sighed morosely and threw the ruined costume back in her bag.

"No, we must be able to come up with something…"

Madeline blurted out several suggestions, but Lori just shook her head.

"It's no use. I'll go down and put my bag in the office."

Lori got up and walked toward the door. She was halfway there when Hanna and Lisa came into the room. The room suddenly got very quiet. The others knew that Hanna and Lisa were Isabelle's fans, and suddenly Lori realized that the two might be involved.

"Have you two seen anything special in here this morning?" she asked them.

Both Hanna and Lisa shook their heads.

"Nothing at all. What's up?" Hanna said, smiling a little haughtily.

Lori just shrugged her shoulders.

"Somebody ruined my clown costume," she said, "and somebody said that they'd seen one of you coming in here earlier. I just thought that maybe you saw something."

Lori was just talking from the top of her head, but she could see Hanna and Lisa exchanging nervous glances. Hanna looked at Linda, who had already changed, and it was so quiet in the room you could have heard a pin drop.

"Admit that you're in on this somehow," Kate said angrily, walking up to the two girls with her face red.

"No, come on," Hanna said angrily, "We didn't do

anything. You're just making that up to be mean. Don't you think we've seen how you're always kissing up to Lori?"

"Kissing up to Lori? Get lost, Hanna!"

Madeline laughed and turned to Hanna and Lisa.

"Just look how you're acting now," Lisa exclaimed sulkily. "You're always siding with Lori, aren't you? She might as well have ruined her costume herself, just to get us into trouble!"

"That really wouldn't surprise me at all," Hanna said, making her way to the bench to change.

Lori was now shaking with anger. She knew that Hanna and Lisa and maybe even Linda were involved, but without proof she couldn't do anything about it. Instead she said goodbye and went downstairs to the office.

In the indoor riding ring, the vaulting was in full swing and Lori sat down with her parents and Paulina, who were sitting on the stands watching. Lori was so angry about the sabotage to her clown costume that she couldn't concentrate on what was happening in the ring.

When Rita asked what had happened Lori told her in whispers. Rita of course was furious. She had worked hard on that clown costume and was as angry and disappointed as Lori.

"Leonard and the other leaders will have to deal with this, won't they?" Rita whispered.

Lori nodded.

"I'll talk to Marianne after the show. I think I know who did it, but of course they won't admit it."

"Just don't accuse any innocent bystanders," Arnold said seriously, and Lori nodded again.

"Of course, but these girls are Isabelle's friends, and I'll bet anything they had *something* to do with ruining my costume."

The advantage of not being in the show was that Lori now got to see everything. The show really was good and everything worked out perfectly.

She was holding her breath when Marianne rode dressage with the beautiful Bianca. Piaffe, passage and extended trot – Bianca did the moves as if they were nothing, and Marianne sat practically unmoving in the saddle. You couldn't see her giving any aids when Bianca did all the difficult moves.

The jumping competition between Catherine on Blackie and Evan on Mistral was exciting. The fences got higher and higher, and each time it seemed as if little Blackie would knock them down. Finally, Evan and Mistral had to give up. The big gelding knocked down a pole at 61 inches, while Blackie just soared over it. The crowd cheered wildly and Catherine got a big bouquet of red roses and a beautiful statue of a horse as her prize.

Lori also saw the parade "The Horse Through the Ages," and her heart ached when she saw Matt ride around on his little Popcorn. She should have been there too. Now she had to sit here in the stands and watch.

When only the pony quadrille was left Lori began

getting a little nervous, and she wondered how the girls felt. They made a magnificent entrance, lining up at the middle line, facing the stands and greeting everybody. Lori bit her nails and prayed silently over and over again that everything would work out.

And lo and behold, everybody managed the entire program without even the smallest mistake! To the strands of an old military march, they managed to ride the two big figure eights in a gallop, change hands across the diagonal and finish facing the stands again.

It was a finale worthy of a great show, and the applause seemed to go on forever. While the ponies and girls were still facing the stands, Karl Fenton made a short speech about The Horse Day, and then it was over.

Lori breathed out. It felt good that it was finally over. She was tired and totally sapped of energy, and she made a face when she remembered that she had promised to lead Pluto for the pony rides.

She knew that the rides were starting soon, but she decided to go to the office first and see if Marianne had time to talk to her.

Luckily, she did, and Lori told her about the clown costume and what had happened. Marianne thought it was a terribly mean thing, and she promised Lori to ask around if anybody had seen anything during the morning. She couldn't do more than that, so Lori thanked her and went to help with the pony rides.

There were people everywhere, and at the pony rides there was a long line of kids and parents. Lori saw her dad and Paulina and waved cheerfully before taking Pluto from the girl who had been holding him.

The Welsh pony nuzzled her hands in a friendly way, hunting for treats, and Lori gave him a piece of carrot.

The line of kids was about two hours long, and during that time Lori got to walk quite a few rounds with the gentle Pluto. It wasn't great fun, but Lori thought about the money coming in for the riding school and that made it easier to bear the tedium.

Paulina fell in love with riding and Arnold had to let her ride three times. He laughed cheerfully at her. It wasn't enough that Lori was riding, now Paulina would probably start too.

After a while, the audience started thinning out and Lori led Pluto to his stall. A lot of visitors were still milling around, looking at the horses, and Lori heard kids nagging about starting to ride.

She smiled to herself. It would be good for the riding school if more kids started.

"Hey, Lori, I have to tell you something."

Lori turned in surprise. Outside Pluto's stall was a little red-haired girl with glasses and a gap between her front teeth. Lori recognized Martina, who rode in one of the beginner's groups.

"Sure, what is it?"

Lori left the stall and looked questioningly at her.

"Can't we go somewhere where there're fewer people?"

"Sure, come this way."

Lori led the way into the ring and up into the empty stands.

"I know who tore your costume apart," Martina whispered and leaned close to Lori.

"Oh? Who?"

"I saw Hanna and Lisa go up to the clubroom, and when they came down Hanna said, 'We sure did that well. There's no way she can ride and be silly now.'"

Lori looked at Martina, who nodded emphatically.

"You're sure that's what you heard?"

"Totally! I felt so sorry for you when I heard that your costume was ruined, it was so beautiful. But I couldn't find you, even though I tried."

"I was sitting here in the stands," Lori said. "Come on! You have to tell Marianne this. She's in the office."

They went to the office, but Marianne was busy and it was quite a while before she could talk to Lori and Martina.

When she finally heard what Martina had to say, she was smoldering with anger and sent Lori and Martina to find Hanna and Lisa. Marianne wasn't going to accept something like that happening in her school. Lori was almost scared when she saw how angry Marianne got.

It wasn't hard to find Lisa and Hanna, but when Lori

said that Marianne wanted to talk to them they were surprised and refused to come along. They didn't come until Lori threatened to go get Marianne.

Lori had wanted to hear what Marianne had to say to them, but Marianne curtly told Lori and Martina to leave the office.

"I'm sorry, Lori. This is between the three of us."

Lori didn't learn what Marianne had told Hanna and Lisa afterwards either, since her parents came to pick her up soon after Marianne shut her office door.

She was so tired that she fell asleep on the way home even though it was just three in the afternoon. It felt strange to go to bed in the middle of the day, but she just had to sleep a little before dinner.

That night she went to bed early and had no idea how she would manage to get up in the morning to work as an official at the riding competitions.

Lori felt a little bad for not visiting Tony, but she comforted herself with the knowledge that George was taking good care of him.

Right before she shut her eyes she remembered that Rita and Arnold had promised to go to the competition tomorrow afternoon to look at Red Top.

Lori didn't think that she really had a shot at buying Red Top, but she couldn't help hoping, and with a smile she fell asleep and slept soundly all night.

Chapter 14

Lori just couldn't understand why her alarm clock went off so early on a Sunday morning, but she got out of bed anyway and went to shut it off. She was tired and felt like a train wreck when she saw that it was just seven AM. In half an hour she and her mom had to leave to pick up Kate, and then they'd all continue to the riding school and the jumping competitions.

Lori looked in the bathroom mirror and made a face. Her blonde hair was ruffled and she looked tired and pale. She heard her mom shutting off the clock radio in the next room. Lori washed, sighed, and then hurried to get ready.

Why had she promised to be an official? Well, it was too late to do anything about it now.

Kate seemed as tired as Lori, and poor Kate had to

participate in both competitions that afternoon. The girls dozed in the car on the way to the riding school.

Things were already bustling inside the stable, and in the indoor riding ring the course builder was finishing the course for the first competition, an Easy C.

The weather improved and lots of horse transporters had already arrived. Lori watched for Gruenwald's trailer, but it hadn't arrived yet. This wasn't odd, since the competitions for big horses weren't until the afternoon.

Finally, the first competition began, and Lori had the opportunity to be the starter. It was an easy job. Once she had waved the horses and riders off she could watch without having to keep count of knocked down poles.

So far, there were only small ponies jumping, and Lori thought they were cute. Their legs were working like drumsticks as they seemed to float over the fences. Sometimes it didn't work too well, since little ponies, like little kids, have wills of their own. More often than not a hopeful rider had to ride out again with a pony that had jumped only one or two fences.

The fences were getting higher and higher, and after about two hours the first competition was finished and a winner was selected. Lori took the time to get a hot dog in the coffee shop during the break. Since she was an official, she had free food and drink for the day.

The next competition was Easy B for ponies and, once

Lori was the starter. The job was a little dull, but
she thought that helping was better than just sitting in the
stands and watching.

Not a minute went by that Lori didn't wonder if and
when Isabelle was going to appear with Red Top, and when
she suddenly heard Isabelle's voice and saw her entering
the stands she drew a deep breath. Here we go, she thought
to herself while absently waving off horses and riders.

The Easy B-class for ponies was a big one, with many
participants in all three categories. Lori followed the
progress of her buddies from the riding school with interest
and was glad when Emma went flawlessly on Tin-Tin and
won her category.

Several other club buddies placed high, and Lori was
really sad that Tony was lame so that she couldn't be in
the competition. It would have been fun to show him off!
He had been training so nicely the week before he got the
sprain that she was sure she would have had a chance at a
ribbon.

When the Easy B was finally over there was a one-hour
break, and during that time Lori walked around looking for
Red Top. She found him tied up in a stall in the guest stable,
with a lead rein that was too short and no hay to chew.

He was as thin and wretched as when she saw him last,
but at least his coat was shining a little more and he seemed
a little more alert.

Lori didn't dare go in the stall with him, as she'd heard that he liked to kick. Also, Isabelle could appear anytime.

Instead, she gave the horse a long and pitiful look and took the aisle past Kariba's stall before she hurried to the coffee shop, where Emma, Madeline and Kate were having a soda.

"Congratulations, Emma!" Lori said, sitting down with them.

"Thanks!" Emma said, smiling.

"Have you been in the guest stable?" Kate asked.

Lori nodded.

"How was Kariba?"

"She was standing calmly in her stall, eating hay," Lori answered and went to get a mug of cocoa.

There was a line for the vending machine, and Lori saw Hanna and Lisa in front of her. They didn't even bother to give Lori a look, and she certainly wasn't going to say hi.

Of course the machine started blinking that the hot cocoa was out just as Lori came up to it. Instead, she had to make do with a cup of lemon tea. It was sweet and not especially delicious, but at least it was hot. The indoor riding ring was cold and Lori's hand and fingers were completely red.

"The riders may go out onto the course!" somebody announced.

Many of the patrons of the coffee shop flew out the door immediately. It was close to one o'clock, and in a few minutes the first competition for big horses would begin. Lori got nervous and rose to her feet to see if her parents had come. After all, they'd promised to take a look at Red Top. Yes, there they were!

They all went up to the stands. Lori didn't have to work as an official during this class. Instead, she sat with her parents and could check out the horses and riders at her own leisure. The closer to Isabelle's starting number they got, the more excited Lori was. When the starter finally called the number Lori felt her mouth go totally dry.

Isabelle trotted onto the course with Red Top, who obediently stopped when she pulled him up to greet the judge. Red Top's head was hanging low and Isabelle sat with her hands high and leathers way too short.

Their starting signal soon came and Lori clenched her teeth. Now! Now her parents would see how badly Isabelle rode.

Red Top started by knocking the first fence down, since he came in all wrong. Isabelle jerked at his mouth to punish him and hit him with her crop. This disturbed the horse, making him come in wrong for the next fence too, but he managed to leap over it although Isabelle nearly fell off.

Red Top broke into a trot. Isabelle straightened again and managed a gallop toward the fences on the diagonal.

"That's not a very beautiful horse," Rita said quietly to Lori.

"I know," Lori whispered in answer, "but he doesn't get the food he needs or anything."

"Isabelle isn't a good rider," Kate said. She was on Rita's other side and had heard Lori's and Rita's whispers.

They fell silent again and watched as Red Top made the next two fences with close calls. He seemed sleepy and listless and Isabelle angrily rapped his shoulder a couple of times. Red Top increased his speed a little and made the fences on the long side a little better.

Isabelle hit him again, and when the last two fences came up Red Top was going very fast and virtually threw himself over them. His eyes were wild and his nostrils shone red when Isabelle stormed toward the finishing line and then suddenly reined him, forcing him to open his mouth and raise his head to avoid the pain.

"Four faults for this horse and rider. The next competitor is Peter Hanson on Tiffany."

Isabelle walked Red Top out of the indoor riding ring with a grim face, and before the door closed Lori heard her screaming in a shrill voice, "Stupid wretch of a horse!"

Lori looked at her parents. What would they have to say about Red Top?

"No, Lori, I don't think that's a good horse," Rita said slowly when they had left the indoor riding ring and were standing outside.

Lori looked down. She didn't know how to explain.

"I think you should look for another horse," Arnold said, patting Lori's shoulder.

"But it's Red Top I want!" Lori exclaimed. "Can't you understand? He's just badly ridden and cared, for and…"

"I understand how sad you are," Rita said, stroking Lori's cheek, "but you have to look for another. We have to go home now because the Pearson's daughter can only babysit Paulina until two."

As Lori's parents walked toward their car, Kate came out from the stands.

"Well, what did they say? Can you buy him?"

"No, Mom and Dad said no way," Lori sighed. "I don't know what to do."

She felt like she was going to cry, and with tears in her eyes she ran for the bathroom to be alone. She didn't know where Kate went and she didn't even care.

Easy C was over before Lori decided to go back. This day hadn't turned out the way she had hoped, and it didn't get any better when she heard Isabelle talking about Red Top's fiasco when she went to the bathroom again later on. Lori was horrified to hear that they were going to try to get a vet to put Red Top down, due to his "moodiness."

Lori slowly walked away. She decided to help build the course for Easy B.

While walking to the indoor riding ring she met George and Sarah, who had come to watch the competitions. Lori talked to them for a while, trying to hide that she'd been crying.

In the ring, everybody was hauling poles, and Lori

worked as hard as she could. Rebuilding the course went quickly and easily, and Lori and the other officials were soon looking out over a new course.

The riders slowly started entering and, in order to avoid meeting Isabelle, Lori went back to the coffee shop.

The shop was almost empty, and she tiredly sat down at an empty table. It was nice to sit for a while and she barely managed to get up when somebody announced that the competition had begun.

There were lots of people in the stands. Lori sat with Madeline and Emma on the first bench. Kate was just riding out. She had failed in easy C, knocking down three fences.

When Kate and Kariba entered the course Lori kept her fingers crossed for all she was worth. This time Kate managed better. Her beautiful Kariba took the fences easily, as if they were nothing, and Kate smiled happily when the speaker announced that their round was flawless.

Just three riders after Kate, it was Isabelle's turn. Lori drew a deep breath when she saw Isabelle and Red Top enter the course. Red Top was already covered with nervous sweat and Isabelle looked angry and stubborn.

This didn't look good. Red Top completely knocked down both the first and second fences. Isabelle tore at his mouth and kicked his flanks, making him advance all wrong for the third fence, a big blue and white oxer.

Lori saw that their run-up was wrong and closed her

eyes in horror. Then she heard a crash and somebody screaming. In the next moment, she looked up and saw horse and rider lying unmoving in a mess of poles. Then, Red Top moved and managed to get up on all fours, but he refused to touch one hind leg to the ground.

Isabelle was lying totally still in the sand and there were several officials around her. Lori quickly jumped the boards and ran over to Red Top. He was standing totally listless with his head hanging and ears straight out. His flanks were covered with wounds from Isabelle's pointed spurs. Lori almost cried when she saw how badly he'd been treated.

"Call an ambulance!" somebody suddenly shouted.

One of the girls immediately ran off. Lori was standing still, stroking Red Top's sweaty neck, but the horse didn't even seem to notice her.

The competition doctor came running with his bag and carefully examined Isabelle. Somebody asked Lori to lead Red Top out, and she slowly started walking toward the doors with him.

Halfway out she met the Gruenwalds, who came running, looking very worried. For a moment Lori felt sorry for them. She was sure they loved Isabelle as much as her own parents loved her, and they must be frightened and worried.

Once Lori was out in the pale October sun with Red Top, she felt herself start to shake. It was all like some kind of weird dream, but the accident inside must have been real, since she was standing there holding Red Top.

The howls from an ambulance woke Lori from her thoughts and she silently watched as two young paramedics jumped out. They quickly produced a stretcher and disappeared into the indoor riding ring.

Lori stroked Red Top's head.

"I wonder how badly hurt Isabelle is," she whispered softly to Red Top, who carefully bent one ear her way to listen to her voice.

At that moment, the paramedics came out with Isabelle on the stretcher. She was lying very still, but she seemed to be conscious.

Her mom jumped into the ambulance, which disappeared with sirens screaming. Red Top shied back frantically, but Lori talked soothingly to him.

James Gruenwald came up to Lori and the gelding.

"You can lead him to the transport," he said, "and I'll take him directly to the vet's tomorrow morning."

"The vet!" Lori exclaimed in horror. "No, please, let me buy him."

"Are you out of your mind? This horse is crazy! Come on now, lead him to the horse trailer and we'll load him."

Lori felt her tears running.

"But I'll pay for him right away. Please, you can't kill Red Top! Can't I call my parents first?"

"Okay, I'll give you five minutes. Then I'm leaving, no matter what you say."

Lori gave him the reins and ran into the office. Marianne was on the phone, accepting late entries for the dressage competition next weekend.

Lori jumped up and down impatiently. Finally Marianne hung up and Lori quickly grabbed the phone, dialing her home number. Her fingers were trembling and the first time she missed a digit. She got hold of herself and dialed again.

"What is it?" Marianne asked in surprise.

"Red Top! He wants to put Red Top down!"

Lori felt tears rising in her throat. Would she ever be connected?

"No!" she moaned. "The line's busy!"

Her tears started running again and she frantically redialed the number. It was still busy and she was sure five minutes had passed now. She had to go out and ask James Gruenwald for more time.

Lori ran out of the office and almost collided with Leonard, who was on his way in. She threw open the door to the yard and ran to the parking lot, where Gruenwald was just backing up his big Mercedes with the horse transport connected to it. He put the car in gear and drove down the road without seeing Lori, who ran after him in despair.

"Wait, wait! You can't!"

Lori stopped, panting and sobbing. The car was already

speeding along the avenue and Lori felt all hope disappear. Her dream horse, the only horse she had ever wanted for her own, was gone.

Feet dragging, she walked back to the guest stable. She wanted to sit down in Kariba's stall to be alone, because she couldn't bear her friends' curious looks when they saw her teary face.

The stable was empty and silent and Lori went into Kariba's stall. The mare looked with surprise at the girl who sank down in a corner and hid her face in her hands, but then the horse went back to her hay. Lori felt as if her heart would break.

Suddenly, the stable door opened and she heard George ask where Lori was. Lori got to her feet and quickly wiped her eyes.

At first, she couldn't believe her eyes. She blinked a couple of times in amazement. Kate came walking in with – Red Top! George and Sarah were walking with them, and they were holding Paulina's hands!

Lori quickly left Kariba's stall and stood gaping in the passageway.

"So there you are," George said, smiling his warm smile.

"Hi, Lori! Here's the surprise of your life!"

Arnold and Rita came into the guest stable.

"But… what… how…"

Lori couldn't get two connected words out, but she

smiled through her tears before she threw her arms around Red Top's neck. The horse nervously shied back from her hugs.

"What happened?" Lori said after a minute.

Kate gave her the reins.

"I'm afraid I don't have time to explain," she laughed, "because I'm riding the jump-off with Kariba in a minute. There are only four horses and riders left. You take him."

Kate quickly led Kariba out and prepared for her jump-off. Meanwhile, George explained that Kate had phoned him, saying that Lori needed his help in case James Gruenwald refused to sell Red Top to Lori's parents.

What had happened was that Rita and Arnold had decided to buy Red Top after all. When Leonard had explained what a nice looking, good riding horse he could be, they had decided to offer two thousand dollars for him.

He was worth considerably less now than before, because he'd been so badly ridden, and Kate, who had seen Lori run into the office to make her phone call, ran after George and immediately bought Red Top for a song. Then she had hurried to the clubroom, called Lori's parents and asked them to come as quickly as they could.

"But our line was busy," Lori said in surprise. "How can you be both here and at home?"

"Honestly, Lori, it must have been twenty minutes since you called," Rita smiled.

"You are the best," Lori said, hugging her mother. "By the way, what happened to Isabelle? Is she badly hurt?"

"Not at all," George said. "Her mom made the paramedics carry her out. She was on her feet in the ring for several minutes before they came with the stretcher, and she seemed just fine. Maybe she's got a slight concussion, and hopefully she's learned something."

"So what are you going to do with Tony?" Sarah said merrily and smiled until the skin around her eyes wrinkled.

"*I* ride Tony," Paulina said confidently, patting Red Top's foreleg, which was the highest spot she could reach.

The horse carefully bent his noble head, nuzzling Paulina, who stroked his muzzle with delight.

"I think the jump-offs have started," George said, looking at his watch. "Let's go cheer for Kate."

"You do that," Lori said. "I'll take Red Top to his stall and care for him. I've been wanting to do that for so long…"

Once the others left for the indoor riding ring Lori unsaddled and unbridled Red Top. She borrowed one of Kate's brushes and carefully started grooming him. She gave him a little of Kariba's hay, to be sure he had something to chew on. He emptied the bucket of fresh water almost at once, and Lori had to run to the tap to refill it.

She carefully let her hand slide down the leg he'd been limping on earlier. It felt just as it should, cool and dry. He didn't seem to be in pain anymore.

Lori thought he'd just hit the leg and there probably wouldn't be any swelling. With relief she sighed, gave her horse a carrot and a goodbye hug, and left him to go watch the prizes being given away.

Halfway to the indoor riding ring she saw that she was too late. Kate was just trotting out with a blue ribbon on her bridle.

"Hey! Lori! We won!" Kate called, making a victory sign with one hand.

Lori drew a deep breath, cupped her hands in front of her mouth like a funnel, and happily shouted back.

"So did I!"